"This unforgettable adventure will bring you to place
beyond your wildest imagination... All aboard!"
Sinéad O'Hart, author of *The Time Tider*

"This is such an exciting, magical adventure, written with
wit and warmth and a wonderfully bold and bolshy heroine.
It feels like an instant classic."
Sophie Cameron, author of *Away with Words*

"Sharply drawn, beautifully observed and with plenty of action and
humour to make the reader gasp and shriek in equal measure."
Lou Abercrombie, author of *Coming Up For Air*

"A brilliantly written and spirited adventure filled with magic,
mystery, peril, humour and some stunning twists and turns that
completely captivated me. LOVED it."
Kevin Cobane, educator

"There is something unexpected around every corner keeping them,
and us, the reader, on our toes in this thrilling adventure story."
Armadillo Magazine

"Fresh, funny and gripping, this will wrap you in its enchantment and
sweep you away, unable to stop until you reach the final page, but then,
having savoured every word, you really don't want it to end."
Jill Bennett, educator

TOURMALINE
AND THE MUSEUM OF MARVELS

This one's for Dan, my firstborn, with all my love x
RL

LITTLE TIGER

An imprint of Little Tiger Press Limited
1 Coda Studios, 189 Munster Road, London SW6 6AW

Imported into the EEA by Penguin Random House Ireland,
Morrison Chambers, 32 Nassau Street, Dublin D02 YH68

www.littletiger.co.uk

First published in Great Britain in 2024

The Forest Stewardship Council® (FSC®) is a global, not-for-profit organization dedicated to the
promotion of responsible forest management worldwide. FSC defines standards based on agreed principles
for responsible forest stewardship that are supported by environmental, social, and economic stakeholders.
To learn more, visit www.fsc.org

2 4 6 8 10 9 7 5 3 1

TOURMALINE

AND THE MUSEUM OF MARVELS

RUTH LAUREN

LiTTLE TiGER

LONDON

Chapter One

Tourmaline picked up a vial of green liquid and glanced at the professor dozing at the front of the science lab. Professor Nyqvist (the latest in a long line of junior professors at Pellavere University bribed or ordered to wrangle an education into Tourmaline's head) had clearly found her day quite trying. Her efforts to stay awake weren't going well and her head was now sagging gently on to the robes folded across her chest.

Tourmaline looked at the Bunsen burner and the round-bottomed glass flask in front of her. The professor's current state was probably for the best. In the weeks since Tourmaline had fallen into the Source of magic on the island of Elsewhere, during a mission to rescue her mother, there had been several unfortunate incidents, over which she'd had no control. If anything untoward was about to happen, it would be helpful if the professor slept through it. She tried to think positively, though. With any luck, she could complete the chemistry test then meet George and Mai in the orchard as planned.

"No magic," she whispered to herself. "Not now." She turned the flame on the burner up, took one more look at the professor (still asleep), and poured the green liquid into the flask of red powder.

Nothing happened.

Which was better than something terrible happening, but not likely to bring about an end to the science test. Tourmaline needed to get on with more important things – like a very different, secret set of experiments that George had been conducting.

She tapped the glass impatiently, then gave the flask a shake for good measure and turned the flame up even higher.

The mixture in the flask, now a muddy sort of colour, began to bubble. This was promising and Tourmaline took heart. "Professor Nyqvist," she said, "I think it's work—"

The liquid bubbled higher, reaching the top of the flask. Tourmaline hastily turned the flame down, but more and more bubbles appeared, multiplying at an alarming rate. The flask was beginning to look ominously volcanic.

Tourmaline didn't have time to do anything about it. The contents of the flask exploded in such a spectacular fashion that they hit the ceiling. Tourmaline shot upright, eyes wide, heart frog-jumping. "I said *no* magic!"

The professor snorted awake, at first dazed and then horrified, as a cascade of noxious-smelling liquid, bubbles and – somehow – gas rained down on the lab. Tourmaline threw a frantic glance round the room for something – anything – that could stop the chaos.

She grabbed a fire blanket and flung it over the flask, but the blanket began to flicker with green flames. Unreasonable and impossible green flames.

Water. She needed water. She rushed to the sink, filled a large flask and threw it desperately in the direction of the green-flaming blanket.

The water never reached the fire. Instead, as it got close, the droplets turned into snowflakes that floated gently down, merging with the sludgy mess that was still shooting from the original flask. Tourmaline threw her hands up in despair. "Stop!"

But the experiment seemed determined to finish what it had started. Tourmaline ducked under the table until the furious noises from the flask subsided, and then stayed there for several seconds longer just in case.

"I have absolutely no idea how you even managed that," said Professor Nyqvist in the stony silence that followed. "Miss Grey, I feel compelled to tell you that I have no choice but to report this to your mother."

Tourmaline scrambled out from under the table and pushed her curls out of her face, which was hot and probably quite red. "She's not here right now."

Persephone Grey, renowned artefact hunter, had gone to a museum to give her professional opinion on one of their artefacts and wouldn't be back until the following day.

"Then I will leave her a note," said the professor. Her jaw was clenched a little too tightly.

"Perhaps I could..." Tourmaline looked round the room. Something thick and lumpy dripped from the ceiling on to the professor's desk.

"Please do leave, Miss Grey," said the professor in a long-suffering tone. The flask gave a sudden warning belch, and Tourmaline fled.

Several minutes later, she was balanced in a makeshift hammock strung between two apple trees.

"And now she's going to tell my mother," said Tourmaline, having finished recounting the incident to her two friends. "I can't go on like this."

"It's better than the thing in the bathroom," said Mai. "That was much worse."

Tourmaline had gone into a student bathroom and, while she was washing her hands at the long line of sinks, water had suddenly started gushing first out of one set of taps and then all of them. The result had been a hasty exit, a fairly large flood, and extensive water damage to a priceless oil painting in the apartments below. This had caused some difficulties for George since the apartments (and the priceless oil painting) belonged to his mother, the dean of the university.

"Just tell Persephone it wasn't your fault," said Mai. "Everyone knows strange things have been happening at

Pellavere lately, and not *all* of them are caused by you."

"They might be," said Tourmaline morosely. "Who knows?"

"Focus on the current experiment, please," said George, who always became quite focused during the serious business of trying to figure out Tourmaline's magic.

Tourmaline sighed and closed her eyes, then opened them, then put her hands behind her head. It was the exact same pose she had been in on *The Hunter* when her hands had glowed, and she'd realized that the Source had done something to her.

"Anything?" asked George.

Tourmaline looked at him. His brown hair was sticking up on the left side as it sometimes did. His pale face was serious and his pencil was poised eagerly over his notebook. He'd been carrying it round, taking careful notes on the experiments – each of which had been conducted in the hope of finding out when Tourmaline's magic would appear, *why* it appeared and what it could do. And none of which, so far, had given Tourmaline any answers at all. Her magic was wild and erratic, and seemingly unpredictable. The only thing it seemed consistently determined to do was ruin Tourmaline's life.

It had been spring when she'd left Captain Violet's wonderful ship, waved off the wild crew of *The Hunter* at the port and returned to the university where she lived with her mother (freshly rescued from the island of Elsewhere) and her friends George and Mai. Since then, her magic had made a habit of showing up only at the very worst moments – like when Persephone had asked her opinion on a new, possibly magical, artefact she'd found. Tourmaline, having reached out to touch the artefact, had seen on her hands the oil-on-water pattern that had been happening ever since she'd fallen into the Source. She'd had to run from Persephone's lab calling out excuses to prevent her mother from seeing the strange light.

Persephone was already keeping the secret that Tourmaline had fallen headfirst into the Source. And she'd been so very worried that Tourmaline now couldn't bring herself to tell her mother that it had *done something* to her. At least not until she and her friends could figure out what it was that it had done.

They'd tried so many things – most recently holding her hands in ice water (she wasn't keen to repeat that) and jumping out of one of the trees in the orchard (always fun, but it hadn't made the magic appear). George had even snuck into her room in the dead of night and crashed a cymbal next to her head. All that had done was make *her* leap out of bed shrieking and *him* run from the room calling "Sorry, sorry, sorry!"

The magic stubbornly continued to withhold its secrets.

Now George's pencil hovered over his notebook.

Tourmaline looked carefully at her hands. "Nothing," she said. "But you know they don't always glow. They didn't just now in the lab."

It was as though the magic *liked* catching her off guard. Or showing up as a glow and then doing nothing. It was as mysterious and obstinate as the island it had come from.

George, who had really hoped that a hammock (as the place Tourmaline had been when the magic first appeared) would do the trick, took a deep, steadying breath and told himself that all great scientific discoveries were preceded by multiple failed attempts. But he was running out of ideas.

Tourmaline, meanwhile, was beginning to wonder if she was just going to have to make a run for it every time there was an incident, which was getting awkward. She wasn't sure how many more times she could claim a bathroom emergency without having to visit the nurse.

Mai glanced over at the high window of the lab, where a light had just gone on. "Maybe you're a ... a light source? You know, with the glowing."

"I'm not a *lamp*," said Tourmaline, really hoping she wasn't.

"Of course you're not a lamp," said George.

"We know that the Source just makes things more *them*," he said helpfully. "Like the rope and its rope-ness, and the pocket watch that could freeze people. The Source didn't give these objects new abilities, it just enhanced the ones they already had."

"What about the cat?" asked Mai. "And your jacket."

"Fitzsimmons teleporting is the very essence of cat-ness," said George. He frowned. "But I'm really not sure about the jacket."

"What's Tourmaline-ness, then?" asked Tourmaline, who was still struggling to balance in the hammock.

Mai and George both thought.

"You're loyal," said Mai.

George started printing carefully in his notebook.

"And I heard someone say headstrong and impulsive the other day," Mai added, seeing that George was taking notes.

"Who said that?" asked Tourmaline indignantly.

Mai's eyes widened and she waved her hand vaguely.

Tourmaline's eyes narrowed. "It was Josie."

Mai shrugged admission. "It was Josie."

Josie knew Tourmaline better than almost anyone else, having looked after her and George since they were both tiny babies.

"What else are you writing?" said Tourmaline, suddenly sitting up and peering at the notebook. George tried to hide the page, but quickly gave in.

Tourmaline sighed. George had written 'thief' and 'liar' in very small letters with a question mark after each.

"I wrote them small because I know it's not very—"

"It's OK, George," said Tourmaline. "Saying things is sometimes lying and taking things is sometimes stealing. It really depends on why, and who you ask."

"Anyway, you barely even steal things any more," said Mai. "Although you do lie."

"Well, I can't be expected to give up *everything*," said Tourmaline.

George nodded his agreement. It would be too much in one go.

They all thought about this for several seconds, then George wrote, in much larger letters, the word 'indomitable' on the list. He glanced up at his friend. "Because you really are impossible to subdue or defeat," he said.

"Mm," agreed Mai.

Tourmaline looked at the list and found she was pleased with it, although she wasn't sure it was really helping with the question of what the Source had done to her.

At that moment, there was a loud tearing sound and the bedsheets that had been used to make the hammock split down the middle. Tourmaline fell straight through on to the grassy ground of the orchard.

George let out a little noise – partly in sympathy for Tourmaline, and partly in mild distress over what Josie would say when she discovered the ruined sheets.

Mai held out her hand and pulled up her friend. Tourmaline straightened her shirt, untied the remains of the sheets from the trees and bundled them under her arm.

"It was worth a try," she said. "One of your better ideas, really."

The experiments, if nothing else, had been very good for keeping her busy. That meant she couldn't spend too much time thinking about Evelyn Coltsbody, her recently discovered, possibly villainous father. He was currently detained in custody by the Agency for the Investigation and Classification of Magical Artefacts (or AICMA) for trying to take over the magical island of Elsewhere.

George nodded sadly. "I'm sorry, Tourmaline."

"It's not your fault, George. But I *have* to stop this happening. If Mai's mother finds out…"

They'd also recently learned that Mai's mother, Emiko

Cravenswood, worked for the AICMA. The Agency were responsible for removing every bit of stray magic from the world. And if they felt that strongly about whisking magical artefacts away never to be seen again, what would they do to a girl who had been submerged in the very thing that had made those magical artefacts in the first place?

"We won't let her find out. We can't." George shook his head, unable to continue with that line of thought.

Tourmaline waved her arms around as best she could with the sheets in the way. "I *know*. Believe me, George. The Agency wanted to destroy a whole entire island. And I'm a whole entire person. I'm never going near Emiko Cravenswood again." She took a deep but not very satisfying breath, looking down at the torn sheets. "I've got to stop the magic, George. Your experiments just aren't working, and if I don't find out how to get rid of it soon, I'm going to get caught."

George tried not to be offended, as this was true.

"Maybe if we knew more about *all* magic," said Mai.

"How?" asked George.

Tourmaline let out a heavy breath. "The Agency are

the ones who know about that. But it's not like I can march into their headquarters and ask."

"Definitely not," said George, relieved that Tourmaline didn't, in fact, want to march straight into their headquarters. He wouldn't have put it past her.

They entered the university building, heading for the sitting room that Tourmaline, George, and, more recently Mai, shared. Tourmaline stuffed the torn sheets into a very old and ornate brass plant stand, which was currently plantless, and then stomped them down with one boot for good measure. George cast an anxious glance around and tugged on Tourmaline's arm urgently as he saw a professor coming down the hallway.

Tourmaline immediately assumed a breezy expression and put her hands behind her back (she'd taken to doing this to keep them hidden in case they decided to glow again) as she strolled down the corridor. "Good evening, Professor Sharma."

Professor Sharma, who had recently been promoted, and whose posture had greatly improved as a result, folded into himself slightly. "Tourmaline. Mai." The professor's gaze dropped to George then bounced quickly away.

George, whose own gaze had been riveted to the floor, sped up until the whole uncomfortable encounter was a few dozen paces behind and he could breathe again.

"I'm not sure he's quite over everything," said Tourmaline.

George had been forced to assert himself with the professor to get the information they had needed to rescue Persephone. He was absolutely certain that there would be no getting over that for quite some time, if at all.

As they reached the sitting room, he considered that maybe Tourmaline's magical abilities had been affected by the chocolate cake that Quintalle Nix had made aboard *The Hunter*. Tourmaline had eaten a large quantity of it just before her hands had started glowing... He was wondering whether they should try chocolate cake when he realized that he was just hungry.

Still, it was worth a try, for science. "Tourmaline, I—"

But Tourmaline had just remembered that Professor Nyqvist was leaving a note for her mother and that it would be best for everyone concerned if she intercepted it. It was not the first time she had done this.

The last time, she had been looking for a report

about Tourmaline's recent efforts in History, sent to her mother by Professor Sharma. He'd taken over the class after replacing Professor Aladeus (who had left the university under a cloud of suspicion after his dealings with Evelyn Coltsbody had been uncovered).

The report hadn't been very flattering, which Tourmaline had expected, what with Professor Sharma's promotion having gone to his head. She'd decided it would be best to handle the situation by feeding the report to the groundskeeper's goat. Tourmaline had thought it might make a nice snack for the goat, and the goat, not being a picky eater, had agreed.

"I have to go," she said quickly. "If my mother hears what happened in the lab she might get suspicious."

"Maybe you should just tell her?" said George, though he looked doubtful. "I thought you were going to talk more now."

"I *will* tell her," said Tourmaline. "Just as soon as I know exactly what it is that I should be telling her." And with that she hurried off.

Tourmaline lingered innocently at the staff pigeonholes until the coast was clear, then rifled through the papers in her mother's cubby.

The note from Professor Nyqvist wasn't there, which hopefully meant she had forgotten all about it. But Tourmaline had already been completely distracted by something else anyway. In among the bundle of post addressed to Persephone Grey was a postcard. It was addressed to *Tourmaline* Grey, which was unusual in itself. Beyond the birthday card from Great-Aunt Heliotrope which would sometimes arrive in spring and sometimes in autumn, but never in winter when it actually was Tourmaline's birthday, this was the first post she'd ever received.

It was a good thing she had got to the cubby before her mother had.

Tourmaline glanced around again, not sure why she was suddenly balanced on her toes, with an alert, ready sort of feeling inside her. The postcard wasn't signed. On it was written a quite simple and worrying and impossible message:

Meet me at the market,
I'll talk to only you,
Find me when it's darkest,
If you want to learn the truth.

I know your secret, Tourmaline.

Chapter
Two

Tourmaline was late to breakfast the next morning and the state of her hair caused one or two raised eyebrows as she rushed into the refectory. Mai was nowhere to be seen, but George was still there.

She made a quick detour to get scrambled eggs then dumped the plate down opposite George breathlessly. The clang of cutlery lowered the previously raised eyebrows into frowns.

"I have something to show you," she said, as gravely as she could with a mouthful of toast.

George straightened. "Something to do with the magic?"

"No," said Tourmaline, frowning slightly. "It's not that. Or maybe it is. It's ... well, here. Look."

She pulled the postcard out of her pocket and pushed it across the table.

George swiped up the card. It had a picture of a quaint market barrow on it, piled high with bright fruit and leafy vegetables.

Tourmaline gestured impatiently so that George would turn the card over, and then chewed determinedly on her thumbnail as her friend inspected it, first with suspicion, then with interest, and then with downright shock.

George (very quietly, almost to himself) read out the writing on the postcard.

He looked up at Tourmaline and said in an urgent whisper, "If you want to learn the truth? Your secret? What – what does it mean?"

"I don't know," said Tourmaline, running out of thumbnail to chew. She thought she did know, and probably George did too, but neither of them wanted to say.

"Who do you think sent it?"

"I don't know," said Tourmaline. It was all she'd thought about since she'd laid eyes on the card. She'd been hiding her secret for weeks but now someone knew? How? Were they going to tell anyone? And what did they *want*?

"Wait a minute," said George, frowning at the postmark. "This came yesterday. Why didn't you tell me last night?"

"I don't *know*," said Tourmaline shortly. It had given her a think-ache trying to puzzle out what the message meant and she hadn't slept particularly well. She looked at the card in George's hands. "What do you think of it?"

"I'm not sure," he said, a little coldly because he was slightly hurt and Tourmaline wasn't doing anything to make it better. "But if whoever wrote it knows your secret, do you think they mean...?"

"I only have one secret," said Tourmaline.

George looked at her.

"I mean, I only have one secret *now*. At least, one secret that matters." She glanced around then said, in the most hushed voice she'd ever used in her entire life, "Does someone know I fell into the Source? How could they?"

George didn't answer.

29

"Do you think it's very bad?" she asked. "That someone knows?"

George's eyebrows suggested he was thinking, that he was worried, and that he didn't know what to do. All of which made Tourmaline start chewing on another of her nails.

"I don't think it's very good," he said.

"No," said Tourmaline, "it's not very good, is it?"

George read the postcard again and then turned it over to frown at the other side to see if that would help.

"What are you looking for?" asked Tourmaline.

"I don't know," said George. "I just thought the picture might be a clue."

"Oh," said Tourmaline, trying not to sound disappointed. She wolfed down her eggs, then glanced up to check if George was still upset over not being shown the postcard as soon as it had arrived.

George frowned deeper then looked up at Tourmaline, whose plate was now empty.

"Anything?" asked Tourmaline.

"Market," George muttered to himself. "What market?" He put the postcard on the table and

Tourmaline pulled it back towards her. As she touched the postcard, her fingers gave a little glow and the picture on the front – the one of the fruit – suddenly changed under her hand. The change was fleeting but so very definite that they both forgot that George was nursing some hurt feelings.

Tourmaline pulled her fingers up as though she'd burned them and stuffed her hands under the table. She didn't ask "did you see that?" because it was very clear from George's astonished face that he had.

"It looked like—" said George. "The picture went all *dark*."

They both stared at the current picture, in which the bright fruit sat on the wooden barrow, a light blue sky in the background.

The picture that had briefly appeared under Tourmaline's hand had been set against a twilight dark sky speckled with stars. The barrow had contained spheres and globes of smoked glass and dark, dried, velvety things, none of which she could identify, but about which she was extremely curious.

"I wish my hand hadn't been in the way and we

could have seen the whole picture," said Tourmaline. She nodded at the postcard. "You try."

"Tourmaline, your fingers were glowy. It must have been your— It was the ..." here he just mouthed the last word, "magic."

"Just try!" said Tourmaline.

George tried, cautiously, but nothing happened, which proved his point (and was also a bit of a relief).

He blinked, touched the postcard tentatively again, then noticed the refectory was now empty and they were in danger of being late for class.

"We'd better go," he said, standing up.

"We'd better tell Mai," Tourmaline said, not moving.

She was clearly realizing something.

"George."

George took a deep breath. When Tourmaline said his name that way, it could mean any number of things, but he knew he would find all of them worrying.

"Just say it," he said.

"Well," said Tourmaline slowly. "The postcard is a magical artefact, and the only people in the university who really know anything about magic are Emiko

Cravenswood and..."

George, whose eyes had grown wider the closer he'd come to realizing what Tourmaline was going to say, suddenly got all the way there. "You can't mean the Living Archive."

The children had visited the Archives only once before, after learning that magic was real and Pellavere was benefitting from it in the form of a pond in the middle of the Archive. The pond had been made, at some point in the distant past, from magical liquid taken from the Source on the island of Elsewhere.

"There's no other choice," said Tourmaline. "Someone *knows*, George."

George's eyebrows looked quite distressed. "But the last time we went to the Archive—"

"I know," said Tourmaline. Tourmaline's accidental wet toes (after a small slip into the pond) had made her lose her memory of her mother for an alarming length of time before it finally came back. But now Tourmaline's accidental wet *everything* was causing even more trouble and showed no sign of going away. Despite George's worries, she really did have no other choice.

"I won't go anywhere near the pond, George. I promise. But I *need* to know what the postcard means. Whoever sent it knows something and I have to find out what it is."

George sighed and looked at the flagstones. "OK," he said. "But we can't tell the Living Archive about *you*, can we?"

"No, of course not," said Tourmaline. "We'll just ask about the postcard. We can go at lunchtime. Are you all right?"

George took a deep breath, then found it hadn't been deep enough. He'd started to feel a little lightheaded. "It's not that I don't want another adventure, it's just that it's all happening a bit too quickly after the last one. I thought I might at least have time to finish the book I'm reading."

Alas, it was not to be.

Chapter
Three

"A *magical* postcard? Let me see it again," said Mai. Tourmaline had muddled her way through a morning of lessons, none of which she could have told anyone the faintest thing about had they asked. Now she, George and Mai were skipping lunch and heading towards the Living Archive.

George, who had regrets about lunch and was certain there would be more regrets to come once they'd entered the Living Archive, said, "You can see the postcard at the same time as the Living Archive. That way *maybe* we can fit in something to eat."

The girls, walking on either side of him, exchanged a glance.

"Sorry," said George. "I'm hungry."

Tourmaline patted her pockets. Finding she didn't have any snacks to give him, she patted George's arm sympathetically instead.

They walked around a mystifying pile of rubble that seemed to have pushed up from underground somehow. Great blocks of the university's foundations had been dislodged and burst upwards.

George and Mai looked at Tourmaline, wide-eyed. Tourmaline shrugged. She didn't have any answers.

As they reached the great, carved doors to the Archive, George slowed.

Tourmaline, who had been expecting this, said, "I *promise* I won't touch the pond. I won't even stand near it." And then, when George actually stopped, "I won't even look at it."

"We shouldn't even know about this place," he said.

"But we do," said Mai. "So there's no point pretending we don't and there's no point not using it, especially as we've come to ask about magic. It's not like we can ask my mother, is it?"

Tourmaline nodded appreciatively. That was logic even George couldn't argue with. The Living

Archive was far preferable to the AICMA ever getting suspicious.

George sighed, and then sighed again more loudly as though the first time hadn't worked.

"OK," he said. "I'm ready now."

Which was when the doors opened, before any of them reached for the great handle.

Mai hopped back as the mass of carved insects on the doors swung towards them, and the Living Archive who had opened the door glared at them. "Are you going to stand there all day wasting everyone's time?"

Tourmaline was almost reassured by the tiny old woman's familiarly terrifying manner until a mass of vines slithered like snakes over the doorframe, clamouring to be let out into the dim corridor.

She took a step back and peered beyond the woman into the cavernous depths of the Archive.

It had been a strange place the first time they had visited, when the pond was working its mysterious magic on the university above and the books had been imbued with the power of the Source. Now, though, it was more than strange.

An eerie wind blew from inside and Tourmaline shivered.

"If you're coming in, hurry up and shut the door." The woman's robes let out a puff of dust as she turned on her heel and stumped off into the Archive. The children looked at each other, then ducked under the grasping vines, stepping on to the soft ground, which was now overgrown with moss and twining ivy that reached for their ankles.

"Please wait," Tourmaline called after the woman. She rubbed her hands up and down her arms. An odd, crackling feeling was making the hairs there behave strangely.

"Let me guess," said the Living Archive, spinning round and swatting at a tendril that reached out at her from a nearby bookshelf. "You just want to ask a few questions? As if I have time for that." She waved her arms at the general state of the Archive.

The Living Archive made it sound as though answering questions was the most troublesome thing in the world. But, Tourmaline reasoned with herself, that was always the case with the woman. So she pressed on.

"Yes, we have several questions. And a postcard."

The Living Archive started loading books on to a nearby trolley. She was reaching into the shelves, fishing around, darting forwards as though she really were trying to catch an elusive fish, and then pulling them out one by one.

"What's happening to the Archive?" asked George. Several other Living Archives he could see were also trying to capture the books.

"I would have thought that was obvious," said the Living Archive. "We are moving out. The last of the pond is about to disappear into the foundations and the effects are becoming a little ... unmanageable." She said the word darkly and as though it didn't really cover what was happening, but she didn't have time to explain this to children. She gave George a particularly withering glare and Tourmaline squeezed his elbow.

"So you're moving all the books?" asked Mai, who was undaunted by the odd glare or two. "Where will you take them?"

"To the library upstairs, of course," said the Living Archive. "They'll probably settle down once they're situated." She glared at the children again. "Although who knows how this will all end now. Are there very many students left?"

There had been several incidents at the university since they'd come back from Elsewhere. An entire botany class had been attacked by the ferns they were supposed to be dissecting and some art students had permanently purple hands due to some unruly ink, among other things. The result had been that a large number of students had gone off to study somewhere less difficult and a lot of professors had followed them for the sake of their nerves.

Tourmaline was sure she was personally responsible for at least half of the disasters that had befallen the various departments so far. Until now, she'd been quite grateful that she could blame it all on the breakdown in the university's magic and stop anyone finding out about her own magic. Looking at the Archive, though, she was thinking that the problems at Pellavere stretched far beyond Tourmaline Grey's personal troubles.

"What will happen to Pellavere without the pond?" she asked. She was thinking of her own insistence that the Source be left on the island of Elsewhere instead of being used to replenish the pond. But what else could she have done? It was clear that the island wanted to protect the Source and that it wasn't there for people to steal and use as they saw fit. That much was obvious from how Elsewhere had trapped Persephone with one of its many defences.

But *not* taking some of the Source and bringing it back to the university had caused problems too. Tourmaline grappled briefly with the idea that her decision might have been a good one for the island but a bad one for the university, and that possibly decisions weren't all good or all bad, but something in between sometimes.

"What happens to Pellavere is for Dean Gramercy to worry about and none of my concern," said the Living Archive. "Now, what do you want? And make it quick. I don't have all day, do I?"

At that moment a tree/bookshelf let out an ominous creaking groan and leaned alarmingly to one side, ejecting one book and entirely hiding another.

George huddled closer to Mai. Tourmaline hastily

pulled out the postcard and thrust it at the woman, who looked at it as though it were a used handkerchief.

"Someone sent this to me," she said. "I think it might be a magical artefact. But what I really need is to find out what the rhyme means."

She took a breath and waved the postcard.

The Living Archive got out her eyeglass, took the postcard gingerly, sniffed it, turned it over, read it, and then gave it back.

The children waited.

Tourmaline cleared her throat.

The Living Archive cleared hers louder. "You need to heed the message," she said.

"Thank you. But what is it?" asked Tourmaline.

The Living Archive rolled her eyes. "It's a postcard," she said.

"I know that," said Tourmaline, in what she thought was quite a patient voice. "But what does it mean? The picture on the front changed but it won't do it again so I think it's a magical artefact that's stopped working. And how are we supposed to heed the message on the back if we don't understand it?"

"*Meet me at the market, I'll talk to only you, Find me when it's darkest, If you want to learn the truth,*" said George, helpfully. He left out the bit about Tourmaline's secret and Tourmaline gave him a little nod.

The Living Archive scowled at him. "I do know how to read, believe it or not. Whoever sent that is talking about the Dark Market, of course."

"Of course," said Tourmaline. "What is that?"

"It's the Dark Market. And if someone wanted to learn about magic, what better place than there? That's enough questions," said the old woman, wheeling her trolley over Mai's foot as she trundled off to another aisle.

"But there's one last question and it's the most important one!" said Tourmaline. She actually had quite a lot of other questions but knew that she had very little chance of getting answers to any of them.

"Where even is it?" she yelled after the woman.

The Living Archive fixed Mai with a glare. "Why don't you ask that mother of yours instead of constantly bothering me? She works for the Agency, doesn't she? Don't they go around destroying that sort of thing?" And with that the Living Archive disappeared into a stack. Several trees suddenly and violently bent and shifted, hiding all trace of her.

"What?" asked Mai. "Ask *my* mother?"

"The Dark Market," said George, in a hushed voice.

"I had a lot more to ask," said Tourmaline, hurriedly stepping out of the path of a mass of crawling vines. Not least, did it really *have* to be Emiko?

"I thought you were very polite under difficult circumstances," said Mai, who was rubbing her foot where the cart had run over it.

"Thanks," said Tourmaline. "I thought so too."

"She was actually quite helpful," said George. "For a Living Archive. Can we get something to eat?" He ducked as a bookshelf/tree suddenly swung round in a wild arc, narrowly missing his head. "I think we should leave. Right now."

Tourmaline took hold of his hand and they ran for the door, George flinching at a sudden, loud cawing that sounded as though a murder of crows were divebombing them. He didn't breathe again until Tourmaline pushed him through the door and shoved it closed.

She was thinking, hard and fast, about what she should do.

"I've never heard of a Dark Market," she said after a moment. "What do you think it is?"

George's hands were on his knees, but at this he looked up. "Somewhere we should probably avoid."

Tourmaline caught his eye.

"If we had any choice," he added. "Which of course we don't since you got the postcard."

George was right. Even if he hadn't intended to make up Tourmaline's mind, that was exactly what he had done. There was only one thing she *could* do now. She really would have to ask Emiko Cravenswood.

"It's somewhere magical," Mai was saying. "Like a real market, but with all the things you saw on the postcard, and you can buy them, and maybe you can get your fortune read there, and *maybe* there are fairground rides and—"

"That sounds more like a circus than a market," said Tourmaline.

Mai turned and grabbed her arm. "Maybe there *is* a circus there too. We'll have to ask my mother."

"WHAT?" said George, very loudly for him. "We can't really ask Emiko. Sorry. I know she's your mother but she can't find out about Tourmaline."

Tourmaline gave Mai a look that said she'd needed a bit more time before telling George that they were definitely going to ask Emiko about the Dark Market. And Mai gave Tourmaline a look that said she should have said so earlier.

Tourmaline steered George quickly towards the refectory and told him in the least alarming way she could think of what was going to happen.

"I really need to eat," said George, suddenly sounding quite faint.

"Don't worry, George. We can do this without Emiko knowing a thing about me," said Tourmaline. She patted his arm absently because she was thinking about other things entirely. What was the Dark Market really? And *where* was it? And why did the mysterious sender of the postcard want her to go there?

Chapter
Four

Tourmaline stood outside Emiko Cravenswood's office and swallowed. She had been avoiding Mai's mother at all costs, to keep her magic secret from the person she least wanted to know about it. She'd have to be *very* careful.

"Do you still want to do this?" asked Mai, concerned. George had already (and quite gratefully, Tourmaline thought) gone off at his stepfather Jacoby's invitation to read a new history journal, saying that he would meet them in half an hour.

Emiko's small office had a modest brass sign on the door etched with her name and underneath it, the title *Administrator*. She wasn't actually an Administrator, of course. The Agency had sent her to Pellavere undercover to find out more about the Living Archive and the mysterious magical pond there. Now she had been assigned the task of keeping an eye on what was left of the pond, which was why both she and Mai were still residents of the university.

Despite not being an actual Administrator, Emiko Cravenswood was widely lauded as the best Administrator Pellavere had ever had. It didn't matter that she was only there to surveil the Living Archive, because everything else was running like clockwork.

"We have to," said Tourmaline.

Mai touched her shoulder sympathetically. "I agree. What if your magic gets worse? Or what if the person who sent the postcard sends another one and someone sees it and finds out? Or what if you *don't* go to the market and whoever it is decides to tell the whole world that there's a magic girl and you get kidnapped by scientists and put in a lab and—"

Tourmaline knocked rapidly, insistently and loudly on the door.

"Come in," called Emiko, and before she knew it, Tourmaline was standing in the most immaculate, organized, catalogued and colour-coded office that she had ever seen.

There was precisely one picture, hung on the wall behind Emiko's desk at the correct angle. It showed a calm and rather lovely meadow – a clearing among some woods. Dappled light fell on the grass and wildflowers.

Professor Sharma was hovering in a corner across from it, looking significantly less calm. Tourmaline widened her eyes at Mai. What was he doing here? But Emiko was waiting expectantly. Tourmaline would just have to get rid of him.

"What can I do for you, girls?" Emiko set aside her clipboard and pushed back her chair. "Please, do sit down." She gestured to the chairs opposite, straightened her suit and perched on the edge of her desk.

Tourmaline sat down. "We've recently learned about something – a place – that we think the Agency wouldn't approve of."

She glanced at the professor to see if this was having the desired effect. He looked mildly panicked to be included in the conversation, but Tourmaline wasn't overly concerned about him feeling uncomfortable since she very much wanted him to leave.

It seemed likely he would – he was already dabbing his upper lip.

She turned back to Emiko. "It's a very ... inappropriate place. I think it could cause a lot of trouble," she added.

"And danger," said Mai. "Terrible danger."

"I should go," said Professor Sharma, trying to gather some neatly stacked papers and dropping them.

"No need for that," said Emiko, although it wasn't clear if she was referring to him leaving or to the mess he'd just made of her efficient paper-stacking.

"No, of course. Quite," said Professor Sharma, but his eyebrows begged Emiko to send help.

"It is magical, though," said Tourmaline, with a severe frown.

The professor made a small dithering noise and then bolted for the door, clutching the papers.

Emiko folded her arms firmly, showing her disapproval of such behaviour. "What is this place, then?" she asked after he had gone.

Tourmaline tucked her unpredictable hands under her legs just in case they misbehaved and pressed them into the chair. They were already starting to sweat.

"It's the Dark Market," she said.

Emiko studied Tourmaline in a sharp-eyed way that reminded Tourmaline very much of Mai, when Mai was still a possible enemy.

"So you *do* know about it?" asked Mai, sitting forwards.

"Where did you hear about the market?" asked Emiko. Her voice was a bit starched.

"Just a – a rumour. Going round the university," said Tourmaline, wondering if Emiko could hear her heart thumping.

"We thought we should report it to the Agency. To you," said Mai, making her expression very earnest and trustworthy. "What kind of place is it?"

Emiko drew in a breath. "The Dark Market is a place where certain types of people can get certain types of items. For a price."

"Do you mean people like Evelyn Coltsbody and Captain Violet?" asked Tourmaline carefully.

"I do."

"And do you mean magical artefacts?" asked Mai.

Emiko made a sound with an ominous tone that

definitely meant yes. "The Dark Market specializes in magical artefacts, among other things."

"What sort of other things?" asked Tourmaline, thoroughly intrigued and on the edge of her seat.

But she got no answer as Mai had asked, "Where is it?" at exactly the same moment.

Emiko sighed a long sigh of deep and longstanding frustration. "We do know how to find it," she said, with a hint of defensiveness. "It's just that it tends to move around. Especially when the Agency tries to find it. Every time an agent gets close, the market is gone."

"That sounds annoying," said Mai.

Emiko blinked. "It really is. The Agency would love nothing more than to shut an operation like that down, but they seem to have some means of detecting us before we can even arrive. I have no idea how they know who we are."

"That's terrible," said Tourmaline.

"Mm," said Mai, as they exchanged a look.

"Someone should do something about it," said Tourmaline.

"Definitely," said Mai.

Tourmaline realized that her hands were going slightly numb under her legs.

"It sounds as though you have something in mind, girls," said Emiko. She seemed wary, but interested.

Tourmaline raised her eyebrows and smiled. "I absolutely do. We need to go and see my mother. I think she can help the Agency with this."

When Tourmaline burst into her mother's study, it was to a welcoming hug and several questions while Mai jiggled impatiently. As soon as Persephone heard about the Dark Market, her face lit up and she thought that the dean of the university would be very interested in the information that such a place existed.

And so it was that Mai, Tourmaline and George (who they'd run into on the way) found themselves heading to the dean's study with Emiko and Persephone to propose a daring plan to all three mothers.

On learning (from snatched whispers on the way) what this plan was, George had gone very pale. Faiza Gramercy's study – which was so imposing it had filled

George with a sense of dread before they even got there – was nowhere near as imposing as his mother herself.

"Do you want to stay behind again?" asked Tourmaline, putting her hand on his back as he slowed down. It had all worked out OK so far and Emiko didn't seem suspicious, but Faiza Gramercy was something else altogether.

"No," said George quickly. "I don't want to be left out. I'm just glad you found me on the way so I don't have too much time to think about it."

Faiza Gramercy raised her eyebrows as Tourmaline, Mai, George, Persephone and Emiko piled into her study. They explained the existence of the Dark Market (Persephone), the importance of shutting the Dark Market down forever (Emiko) and then the possibility that it might be a very good idea if *someone* were to go to the market to achieve all this (Tourmaline).

"I wonder," said Tourmaline, as though she were only just considering the idea, "if something at the market might be able to help with the situation here at Pellavere?"

The dean had listened carefully, sitting behind her desk, deep frown lines on her face and her fingers steeled under her chin. At this, she perked up and gave Persephone a significant look.

"You know," said Tourmaline, "since the trip to Elsewhere wasn't any help."

The children and Persephone had thought it best to tell Faiza Gramercy very little of the truth about what had happened on the island, just in case she got any ideas about strongly encouraging Tourmaline to reveal its current whereabouts.

"You really think," said the dean, addressing Persephone, "that this expedition could help?"

"I do," said Persephone firmly.

"So do I," said Tourmaline, who hadn't been asked, but who had every intention of attending.

Persephone looked at her daughter in surprise. "Do you think that this is one of those hunts that we might go on ... together?" she asked.

Tourmaline tried not to beam in triumph and actually succeeded (mainly because she now felt very guilty about tricking her own mother).

She and Persephone had agreed, on the voyage back from Elsewhere, that they would like to spend more time together, doing something Tourmaline had discovered they both loved – adventuring.

The plans being made now *did* mean that mother and daughter would be together. Which was what Tourmaline told herself so she didn't feel too bad about the truth – that she wanted to go to the market for a secret and very different reason all of her own.

"And will you be accompanying Persephone on this mission?" the dean asked Emiko.

Emiko looked as though she'd like nothing more.

"She can't," said Mai quickly. "If they know an AICMA agent is coming, the market will disappear immediately. It's a whole thing."

The dean looked impressed. Emiko did not.

"But I could go," said Mai, shooting a sideways glance at Tourmaline, who nodded encouragingly. "As a sort of stand-in," Mai said to Emiko. "To make sure the – the protocols are followed."

Tourmaline nodded harder. Protocol was one of Emiko's favourite words.

"I'd be happy to look after her," said Persephone. "It's so nice that Tourmaline has another friend."

Emiko smiled warmly. "And I'm so glad that Mai—"

"I think that this all sounds like an excellent opportunity for the university," said the dean, standing up from her desk to dismiss them before this went on much longer. She caught Emiko's sudden startled expression and hurried on, "That is to say, an excellent opportunity to put a stop to any more flagrant use of magic."

"I quite agree," said Emiko. "Perhaps with Persephone leading the way, we can finally pinpoint the location of the market for long enough to infiltrate it. Then the Agency can swoop in, confiscate all these terrible magical items and almost certainly make a whole slew of arrests." Her face was flushed with excitement, as though it had actually been her idea and not Tourmaline's.

"I – I should go too," George suddenly burst out.

"Yes," said Tourmaline, who could feel that he was quivering. "It would be very useful to have George with us. He's read a *lot* of books."

"He's good at ideas when you need them," Mai added.

George stopped quivering and held his head up.

"I really do think I should go," he said firmly.

Tourmaline found his hand and squeezed it so hard that he winced. This was going even better than she had hoped.

"It's out of the question," said Faiza Gramercy. "Absolutely not."

George visibly wilted. "But—"

"George, I believe I made myself perfectly clear. Now if you don't mind, given the recent ... difficulties and ... incidents ... I have several avenues to explore..."

She sat back down, bent her head over the papers on her desk again, and didn't so much as look up when Emiko opened the study door and Persephone herded the children back out into the hallway.

Chapter
Five

"I'll need to contact the Agency," Emiko was saying to Persephone as they hurried down the hallway ahead of the children.

"Of course," said Persephone, though she sounded as if she wasn't really listening. "I'll have to prepare something suitable from the Stables."

"The higher-ups will want to organize a whole operation," said Emiko. "But naturally, we at the Agency are used to doing such things extremely quickly. And we have been keeping tabs on the market for quite some time now."

"Yes," said Persephone vaguely. "Supplies for three people, and we'll need a cover story." Suddenly she looked across at Emiko. "This is all quite thrilling, isn't it?"

Tourmaline glanced at Mai, and then at George, who was between them, his head down, his hands in his pockets.

"We'll think of something," she said.

"What?" said George, with absolutely no hope whatsoever.

The sound of his voice made Tourmaline's heart squeeze in her chest.

Mai shot her a distressed look over George's head. Her eyebrows, which should have been triumphant, were instead anguished.

"We could... You could..." Tourmaline shook her head to see if any last-minute ideas would come loose. She wasn't sure it was even *possible* to have an adventure without George to share it.

"But I *need* you," she burst out finally. "How can we—" She broke off, sending a furtive glance at Persephone and Emiko, who were still talking. What she wanted to say was, how can we work out what the postcard means and who sent it without the amount of cleverness only a George has? How can we go to the Dark Market and try to stop the magic that is ruining my life when George has to stay behind?

But she couldn't say any of that with an AICMA agent and her own mother right in front of her. So she squeezed George's arm, sighed, fiddled with a loose thread on her shirt and sighed even louder.

"What is it, Tourmaline?" asked her mother, casting a glance over her shoulder. Her face had been alive with the energy she always exuded when she was about to go on a hunt, but it softened at the sight of the three children's faces.

"I'm sorry that George isn't allowed to go," she said. "Maybe Faiza will change her mind for next time? We'll be back before you know it, anyway, George."

Tourmaline frowned. All this was obviously meant to make them feel better, which was nice but didn't actually work.

Persephone consulted her watch. "Goodness, it's late," she said. "And I have so many preparations to make." She glanced sideways at Emiko and seemed to decide something. For a second, there was a furtive look on her face that Tourmaline didn't understand, and then it was gone. "Tourmaline, Mai, I suggest a sensible pair of trousers, some sturdy boots and a warm jacket. When you're ready, meet me by the main gate. We leave at 10 p.m. sharp."

Emiko nodded her approval of this prompt and efficient plan. "I'll contact the Agency, inform them of this operation and obtain the current location of the market," she said, walking away briskly.

Tourmaline looked down at her clothes. She was already wearing sensible trousers (with an abundance of pockets). She was about to point this out but Persephone had gone too.

"George," said Tourmaline.

"I have to go," said George, looking thoroughly defeated. "I just thought of something I have to do."

And he walked away in the same direction as Persephone, leaving Tourmaline looking after him and feeling oddly heavy when she should have been bouncy light.

"Maybe it's better if he doesn't see us off," said Mai quietly.

Which was when Tourmaline fully realized that she was going to have to do this without George by her side.

It was almost dark when Tourmaline emerged from the university building into the quadrangle where Mai was already waiting. Her eyes were bright, her trousers were almost entirely clean and she had a bulging satchel.

"I brought supplies," Tourmaline said, pulling open the satchel to reveal sandwiches, a large quantity of cake and an apple, which Josie had put in there and which Tourmaline had allowed because there was already so much cake.

Mai made an approving noise and they hurried out through the arches and on to the long drive that led down to the external gates of Pellavere. Tourmaline glanced up at the clock tower. It was almost 10 p.m.

"What if your magic does something while we're with Persephone?" asked Mai.

"I'm trying not to think about it," said Tourmaline.

The clock struck as they reached the gates. They were extremely tall and stately and topped with curlicues and a crest, as befitted Escea's finest university. (Or formerly finest university. Tourmaline wondered if it qualified any more.) They were also locked.

Tourmaline gave the gate an experimental push. Definitely locked.

Mai looked up at the curlicues doubtfully. "Persephone did mean these gates, didn't she?"

Tourmaline opened her satchel, took a slice of cake for herself and silently handed one to Mai. "Did you see the odd look on her face when she told us to meet her here? It was as though she was trying to hide something."

"I did," said Mai, through a mouthful. "How do you think we're going to get to the—"

A strong draught blew Tourmaline's curls into her eyes and a shadow fell over the two girls. Tourmaline looked up, then across at Mai to check that her friend was seeing the same thing. Mai's mouth was open.

A large ship-like shape hung in the air above them. It was hard to make out, since it was a mottled bluish-greyish-purple with wisps of white along its sides, which was very close to the current appearance of the sky itself. More visible were the several portholes along the side. They were glinting in the light of the large lamps set on either side of the university gates that had just come on against the darkening evening.

"What—?" said Mai, but words failed her.

Tourmaline looked up beyond the ship-ish thing and noticed that several fine threads attached to it led to a vast balloon above it. The silk rippled and a few stars popped out on the fabric.

Just then, a face appeared at one of the portholes, the round glass swung open and Persephone called out, "Ahoy, there!"

Tourmaline made a sound that was partly astonishment but mostly delight.

"Permission to come aboard?" Mai called up into the sky.

"Permission granted," said Persephone. Two doors opened on the back of the ship and a rope ladder unrolled, touching down next to Tourmaline.

She adjusted her satchel (that much cake was surprisingly heavy), shoved the remains of the slice she was holding into her mouth and grabbed hold of the ladder.

"I think I know," said Mai softly, "why Persephone asked us to meet her at the gates. Away from the university, where my mother is."

"And I think," said Tourmaline, "that you are exactly right."

Tourmaline scrambled up the ladder, followed by Mai and they both rolled, out of breath, on to the floor of the airship.

Persephone closed the doors, stepped quickly to the front of the ship – as though she were in great hurry to get going – and thrust a large lever forwards.

There was a jolt, then the balloon glided through the night air, carrying the ship and its three occupants away from Pellavere.

The inside of the ship had bunks along the sides and a wheel at the front that Persephone was now using to steer it. Tourmaline pressed her face to a porthole and watched the road that led to Brenia city and which she and George had travelled along on a stolen motorcycle several weeks ago. It looked like a grey ribbon laid along a broccoli field of trees. And it made her remember all over again that George wasn't there. She didn't think she'd ever been this far away from him in her whole life. Although he probably would have been less delighted than she was to be this far up in the air.

Mai sidled up close to Tourmaline and said, very quietly, "I think that maybe a lot of magical artefacts were involved in the making of this vehicle."

"I'm sure," said Tourmaline, a lot less quietly, "that the threads attaching this thing to the balloon thing are spider silk from Elsewhere."

She went to stand at the front of the ship next to her mother and looked at her sideways. "What *is* this ship? Where did it come from?" In front of them was a large window and beyond it, on the ground below, a patchwork of farmland, darkly dotted with livestock.

Persephone cast a slightly furtive glance at her daughter. "I *was* going to tell you," she said. "But then you came to me about the Dark Market and there just hasn't been time."

On the way home from the island of Elsewhere, Persephone had decided that she wouldn't keep any more secrets from Tourmaline. Tourmaline had considered making the same promise, but had stopped herself, which she was very glad about now. She thought of her own recent behaviour when it came to telling the whole truth – especially the disaster that was her magic – and decided to ignore Persephone not mentioning the ship right away.

"That's OK," she said.

"This is what I was doing on my most recent trip," said Persephone, and then, as though she had remembered something, "How did your science test go while I was away?"

"Fine. Normal," said Tourmaline quickly. She wondered if Professor Nyqvist might have left by the time she got back, like so many of the other professors. It would save her the trouble of explaining the incident in the science lab.

"Anyway," said Persephone, "a hunter I know at another museum asked me for my opinion on a particularly large and potentially magical artefact." Here she gestured at the ship. "They couldn't work out how to attach the balloon to the ship and it seems that I had a little thread from the island left in my pocket when we left. I thought it might present the perfect solution. Of course, they were only too happy to lend it to me after that, except that..."

"Except that what?" asked Tourmaline.

"Well, I might have promised them that I'd keep my eye out for a certain magical artefact while we're at the Dark Market in exchange." She cast an apologetic glance over her shoulder at Mai, who shrugged cheerfully.

"I really do believe," said Mai, "that the world is better with a little magic in it."

Tourmaline opened her mouth to say that there were rules about this sort of thing and then missed George even more. He would have known the right thing to say about magic not getting into the wrong hands. It was all still a bit tangled in her own head.

Persephone glanced across at her daughter. "Speaking of magic, you are OK, aren't you?"

Tourmaline had noticed a worried line furrowing itself between Persephone's brows ever since Tourmaline had fallen into the Source. It was there now and looking alarmingly deep.

"Of course I am," said Tourmaline. It wasn't a complete lie. She herself was quite all right. It was the things that happened around her that were difficult. "There's no need to tell Emiko. Ever."

"Good," said Persephone. "Not that I'm keen on lying, but I think in this case, a strategic omission is in order. If you're perfectly fine, there's no need for the Agency to know about your little slip."

It had been less of slip, Tourmaline thought, and more of a long fall that ended in complete immersion. But Persephone's concerned smile convinced Tourmaline to smile back reassuringly.

Persephone patted Tourmaline's shoulder. "I just want to keep you safe."

"I'm perfectly safe," said Tourmaline. But she had to blink twice to stop her gaze shooting over to her satchel. She'd tucked the postcard in underneath the cake.

The scenery below had changed to a large city with spires and cobbled streets and many twinkling lights. Persephone smiled and the worried line between her brows went away. "I just wanted to check. It *is* quite soon after the last adventure, and that ended with a lot for you to think about."

Tourmaline thought about the rescue mission to Elsewhere, learning that magic was real and, what was more, responsible for the success of the university she called home. And possibly even more shockingly, finding out that her previously unknown father was none other than the infamous Evelyn Coltsbody. He had caused a lot of problems trying to take over the island of Elsewhere. He'd wanted to use its magic to put himself in charge of Escea and possibly the whole world.

Tourmaline had been preoccupied with keeping her magic a secret in the last few weeks, but that didn't mean she didn't have occasional creeping thoughts about her father, who was currently tucked safely away in AICMA custody.

"No matter what Emiko might think, Evelyn isn't *all* bad," said Persephone quietly.

It was as though she had read Tourmaline's mind.

"Really?" said Tourmaline hopefully. She'd been wondering whether or not he made a difference to how good or bad Tourmaline herself was since *he* seemed to skew quite alarmingly to the bad side.

"No, of course not," said Persephone. "Not many people are entirely bad. And after all, he helped to make you, and you're perfect."

Tourmaline looked out of the window and then

down at the floor. She wasn't perfect. In fact, she was keeping something from her mother right now. It wasn't the first time she'd done it and, truth be told, she was pretty certain it wouldn't be the last.

Persephone gave Tourmaline the sort of adoring look that mothers give daughters, then looked down at a river sparkling in the moonlight. She made an adjustment to a brass dial on the controls. The airship glided on a little further and then came to a smooth halt.

Tourmaline leaned forwards, her hands on the walnut control panel at the front of the ship. Mai came hurrying forwards, a few cake crumbs falling from the front of her shirt.

"This is it," said Tourmaline. She was looking down at the scene below, excitement fizzing in her voice. "We've found the Dark Market."

Chapter Six

The children looked down through the window of the airship. In front of them was the market, the only light for miles around. Dark fields spread off into the distance beyond it. Not far away, Tourmaline could just make out a farmhouse along with several outbuildings. Some of the fields had barns in them and one had a herd of cows, mostly patchwork shapes sleeping under dark trees.

The market itself was softly lit by lamps. It was a large and perfect circle in the centre of a vast cornfield, and it somehow managed to be in the middle of the tall corn without having disturbed a single stalk around it.

"Magical!" said Mai.

"Fascinating," said Persephone. She gazed down for a long moment while Tourmaline fidgeted and exchanged furtive glances with Mai, who was bouncing on her toes.

"I'll land just over there," said Persephone, taking the controls again.

The ship bumped gently against the ground next to a dark barn, then settled. Tourmaline immediately grabbed her satchel and opened the doors.

"Just a minute," said Persephone. She held out a torch for each of them. "Now we can go."

"Wait!"

At the muffled sound from the back of the ship, all three of them spun round, Persephone pulling both Tourmaline and Mai behind her in the doorway.

From under one of the lower bunks, a rolled-up blanket emerged (with some difficulty) followed by a red and sweaty face.

"George!" Tourmaline rushed over, tugging at the blanket until all of George was untangled.

He stood up, looking hot, untidy and extremely guilty. His face was flushed and his eyes were wide. He gave an excited sort of laugh but he was glancing nervously at Persephone.

Tourmaline threw her arms around him and

squeezed until he gasped.

"What are you doing here?" she asked. "How did you get on board? How did you stay quiet all this way? George!" She was so pleased she took his shoulders and shook him, hard. "I thought I was going to have to do this without you."

"I-I sneaked in with the provisions. I'm very sorry, Persephone," said George, sounding truly agonized.

"It's fine," said Tourmaline. "It's more than fine. It's the best thing that's ever happened."

"I wouldn't go that far," said Persephone drily. "But I think that anything I could say right now will pale into insignificance compared to what George's mother is going to say when he gets home. And since time is of the essence here, we had better get going. This can be dealt with later."

"But George is coming with us, isn't he?" asked Tourmaline, linking her arm with his.

Persephone sighed. "I suppose he'd better, now that he's here. We can't very well leave him alone."

"Excellent," said Tourmaline, completely ignoring the fact that Faiza Gramercy would be furious and that

Persephone Grey wasn't pleased – mainly because she herself was absolutely delighted. And George would worry about the consequences enough for both of them.

Tourmaline switched on her torch and towed George out of the ship before anyone changed their mind. But as they pushed through the corn, which was taller even than Mai, Tourmaline got an odd feeling in her stomach. It wasn't exactly excitement and it wasn't quite anticipation. It came close to both, but was mixed with curiosity and a small amount of worry. She pushed her free hand into her satchel and felt for the postcard at the bottom.

Persephone was fiddling with something from one of her pockets.

"What's that?" asked Mai.

"This?" Persephone held up a small bottle of cloudy blue glass. "Emiko gave it to me to contact the Agency once we're inside the market."

Mai frowned. "I've never seen anything like that before. How does it work?"

Persephone shrugged. "Apparently I put the message I want to send into the bottle and someone at the other end with a matching bottle will get it."

Tourmaline suddenly stopped walking and let go of George's arm. "That sounds," she said, "a lot like a magical artefact."

"But it can't be," said George.

"I really think it is," said Mai.

"Do you mean to say," Tourmaline said slowly, "that the Agency for the Investigation and Classification of Magical Artefacts is using *magical artefacts*?"

Tourmaline found that she was 1) extremely interested in trying out the artefact for herself, and 2) absolutely outraged. "But—?" she said. "How can they do that when they only exist to— And after what they wanted to do to the island of Elsewhere? I—" She planted her hands on her hips, snorted in disbelief, and shook her head. "There's a word for that," she said, turning to George.

"Hypocritical," said George, sounding quite certain and even a little bit fierce. "It's hypocritical."

"Yes, that's it," said Tourmaline.

Persephone took a philosophical breath. "I've often found," she said, "that the people who shout the loudest about their beliefs are doing so to cover something up. Sadly, they're also the type of people who are often in charge."

George's face now looked as though he'd just absorbed an entirely new kind of worry. "Maybe there should be different people in charge, then?"

"Probably," said Persephone, smiling at him kindly now. "Come on, there's no time to waste."

She strode off ahead and, after a second, Tourmaline followed her.

As Persephone tucked the little bottle into one of her pockets, Tourmaline caught up. "Do you think it will work? That the Agency will actually be able to get here?" she asked.

"I don't know," said Persephone, looking intrepid. Her excited expression suggested she was much more interested in the magical artefacts she was about to see.

Tourmaline matched her mother's stride and Persephone glanced across at her. "We should do this more often."

"Really?" asked Tourmaline.

"You're old enough now," said Persephone. "And we

did agree that we would."

Tourmaline hoped very hard that her magic wouldn't make an appearance any time soon. It was perfectly satisfying in every way to be striding through a cornfield in the middle of the night on the hunt for magic with the most famous artefact hunter in the world, who just happened to also be her mother. Then suddenly, she stopped.

They had reached the market.

It had been silent while they were walking but now, as they stood at its edge, the market was alive with sound and colour and movement. Vendors called out their wares, customers milled between stalls in lively conversation or haggled loudly over goods. There was the clink of coins and the rustle of tissue paper and bags, laughter and shouting and several types of music all vying for attention.

A path of corn lay in front of them, flattened underfoot like a woven mat, and stalls, barrows and tents stretched away in a curve around the outside of the circle. More carts and tiny stalls filled the centre. The little tents were made of striped canvas and bright silk, held up with poles of polished wood and silver and gold. The barrows had coloured flags and streamers and the stalls had banners flying overhead.

Persephone turned off her torch. "If anyone asks, I am a rogue hunter, looking for magical artefacts for my wealthy and enigmatic employer," she said. Her face was pink with excitement and her eyes sparkled. "You are my trusty, if young, crew."

"I'm a rogue hunter?" said George faintly.

"The fiercest and most roguish," said Persephone.

Tourmaline and Mai exchanged a delighted glance.

George swallowed.

Persephone took a step forwards. "Stay together," she said. "Follow me."

Tourmaline tightened the strap on her satchel. "Does it look darkest, like the postcard said?" she asked Mai and George in an undertone. Her heart was beating fast at the thought of coming face to face with whoever had sent the postcard. Was it somebody she knew, or a stranger? "It's definitely quite dark, but does it get darker? What if it's already *been* darker than this? What if—?"

George's stomach growled loudly. Tourmaline sniffed the air. She could smell something sweet and nutty and probably delicious. "You're right, George. There might be snacks too. We just have to get in there."

They walked past a stall that had an array of jewellery laid out on velvet trays – necklaces with coloured stone pendants that shone with an eerie light and brooches in the shape of animals. There were game sets of carved crimson glass on chequered boards and decks of card with painted figures in strange floating clothes.

The dark interior of one tent was lit by trays of tiny glass bottles, each of which glowed dimly. Next to the bottles was a small cart. Wonderfully fragrant steam rose from it and the man behind the cart smiled at George, who tugged on Tourmaline's sleeve as he eyed the roasting chestnuts.

Persephone was already looking at the next stall down from the cart. Tourmaline had slowed to look at the glass vials and she knew from experience that an un-hungry George was much more focused than a hungry one. A hungry Tourmaline wasn't much better. She fished around in her pockets and found a single coin (the one which had once belonged to Professor Sharma, and at another point to Captain Violet).

"Don't use that," said George, hastily pulling a few coins and some fluff from his own pocket. "That coin doesn't exactly," he tilted his head down and lowered his voice, "belong to you."

Tourmaline pondered this. The coin was in her hand and she wasn't sure who else it could belong to at this point in its history. But George had already paid, so she stuffed it back into one of her pockets.

The man behind the cart was very tall. He had quick hands that made George's coins disappear and three paper bags twisted at the top appear. "Very wise, young man," he said. "That coin is almost certainly a magical artefact."

Tourmaline blinked. "Really? What does it do?" The coin had never done anything before.

"May I see it?" asked the man.

Tourmaline retrieved it. The man took the coin, peered at it more closely, flipped it over and then bit it.

George covered his mouth in horror. Who knew where it had been, except in Tourmaline's pocket, and that was bad enough.

"I couldn't say for sure," said the man. "But it's often luck with coins. Meaning that it improves the owner's luck if they make a wish on it."

He handed it back to Tourmaline. "Thank you," she said politely but, since she'd had the coin for some time, she privately thought that magical artefacts weren't that effective after all.

George paused with his hand in his bag. "They're not ... they're *just* chestnuts, aren't they?" he asked the man dubiously. "They don't *do* anything?"

The vendor smiled down at George. "Guaranteed to be delicious and nothing more," he said.

"I thought everything here was magical," said Tourmaline.

The man shrugged. "I've found over the years that people prefer a reliable snack over one with unknown effects. The clothing stall over there is non-magical too. People like magic, but they draw the line at magical trousers. Are you here looking for something in particular?"

"We're hunters," said Mai. "Our captain is looking for magical artefacts. She's very fierce. We all are."

She looked to George for confirmation. He nodded and did his best to look fierce.

Tourmaline had tipped her bag up into her mouth and then had no choice but to chew with her mouth open because the chestnuts were roasting hot. She cast a quick glance in Persephone's direction, but her mother was deep in conversation with the owner of the stall next door.

"We've come to learn about magic too," she said, once her burnt tongue was working again. "So we'd like to talk to someone who knows all about it."

"If you don't mind me saying," said the man, "that's a little vague."

Tourmaline looked at her friends. She hadn't been sure how much to say, but the man was right. Mai gave her an encouraging smile. George widened his eyes and shook his head. And Tourmaline decided that, on this occasion, George was right. She hadn't told her own mother about her magic or the postcard, so it didn't seem right to blurt it out to the first person she met at the market, even if he was very good at roasting chestnuts.

At that moment, she spotted something that grabbed her entire attention. She nudged George and then Mai without taking her eyes off it.

"Never mind," she said to the man. "I think I've found what I was looking for." Her skin prickled with excitement and apprehension.

"Oh!" said Mai. "It's—" She cut herself off, casting a glance around.

Tourmaline had spotted the barrow from the postcard. The very same one that she'd made appear with her magic.

Chapter
Seven

The barrow was further along the curve of the path. It was definitely the one from the postcard, although the goods on it looked a little different to how they had on the picture. Behind the barrow stood a smiling woman with red hair curled almost as tightly as Tourmaline's own.

Tourmaline hurried towards her, dodging round a group of people wearing long robes who were speaking a language she had never heard before. Mai, whose paper bag was already half empty, turned round to say goodbye to the chestnut-cart man. But though the cart was still there, the tall man behind it had suddenly disappeared. Mai frowned.

Tourmaline strode off ahead, all her thoughts bent on finding out who had sent the postcard and how she could stop her magic before it ever showed up again. The answers were right there within her grasp and the thought made her break into a run.

When George and Mai caught up, Tourmaline was frowning in a puzzled way at a sign hanging on the front of the barrow. Its spidery black lettering read:

PAYMENT VIA SECRET ONLY.
NO COINS, OATHS OR TREASURE MAPS.
NO EXCHANGES OR REFUNDS.

George nudged her arm. Fanned out on a tray was a stack of the very same postcard that she had tucked into the bottom of her satchel.

"Oh!" said Tourmaline. Her heart gave a furtive bump and she checked that Persephone was still back at the stall. She was about to find out who had sent the mysterious postcard. Maybe it was the woman standing right there behind the barrow currently serving another customer. Tourmaline studied her face and her tightly curled red hair. She didn't look at all familiar.

Mai riffled through the tall stack of postcards.

There were several different designs.

"That's a very popular item," said the woman, who had finished with the other customer. "If you need to get a subtle yet magical message to someone it does the job perfectly."

"Have you sold one of them recently?" asked Tourmaline. "Or – or sent one?"

The woman laughed. "Sent one? No. But I've sold at least seven of them tonight. They're one of my best sellers. Would you like one?"

"No, thank you," said Tourmaline, her heart sinking. Anybody could have purchased one and sent it to her.

"Do you see anything else you like?" The woman was still smiling at Tourmaline in a friendly way.

"I like all of it," said Tourmaline, looking at the trinkets and wondering what each of them did. But as fantastic as the magical artefacts were, they weren't what she needed. She gestured to the sign on the front of the stall. "Payment via secret? What does that mean?"

"It means your coins are of no use here," said the woman. "You can keep them for yourself and all you need to do to take one of my items home with you is tell me a little secret."

George tugged surreptitiously at Tourmaline's sleeve to let her know he thought this was a strange arrangement. Tourmaline pulled her arm away. She didn't have any coins except the lucky one, anyway.

"But secrets aren't valuable," said Tourmaline. She had several secrets, and although they were sometimes troublesome and sometimes necessary (and in her case recently, very large and difficult) she'd never thought of them as valuable.

"Then consider my magical artefacts a gift in exchange for something that means little to you," said the woman.

Tourmaline wasn't sure what to say to this. "I'm not really looking for a magical artefact," she said. "I want to learn about magic itself."

The woman raised an eyebrow. "So it's something less tangible you want," she said.

"I want to know how magic works," Tourmaline clarified, in case she was being too vague again. "What it can do and how to control it. So it only works when you want it to and you can make it go away if you want."

The woman spread her arms wide. "Then you've come to the right place. There's just the small matter of payment first." Behind her, there was a little tent, and she swept aside a flap and gestured for Tourmaline to follow her inside.

Tourmaline popped the last of her chestnuts into her mouth to see if it would help with the fact that she felt suspicious.

She turned to her friends and said quietly, "Do you think she's going to help me?"

"I'm not sure you should tell her a secret," George whispered.

"But I *have* to stop the magic, George. And we came all this way." She glanced at the woman and lowered her voice even further. "What if she *is* the one who sent the postcard to me and she doesn't want to say so out here?"

"Then you should be very careful," said George promptly. "We don't know what the postcard-sender wants."

Mai ducked a little to put her head close to the others. "Who says it has to be a real secret? Just make one up."

"That's a brilliant idea," said Tourmaline, brightening. "What can she possibly use secrets for, anyway? They're not worth anything."

George frowned. "Maybe they are. What about the postcard? It said someone knows *your* secret. And unless she's the one who sent it and she already knows, you can't tell her that."

"Well, of course I won't tell her *that*," said Tourmaline, mildly offended.

"Are you ready?" asked the woman. She shouldn't have been able to hear them talking but suddenly Tourmaline wondered if she had.

"I think so," said Tourmaline.

"Then come with me," the woman said, beckoning her into the tent.

Tourmaline looked at each of her friends and went in with her heart bumping at the strap on her satchel. Inside the tent was dimly lit with strings of yellow lights. A small round table stood in the middle, with a chair either side. On the table was a small carved box that Tourmaline really hoped wasn't made of bone.

The woman let the flap of the tent fall and all the

noise of the market stopped immediately. "Please, take a seat," she said.

"Thank you," said Tourmaline, trying not to feel like she'd suddenly been whisked away from her friends and taken somewhere else entirely.

The woman sat down, carefully opened the box (it was empty) and looked at Tourmaline expectantly.

"What's that for?" she asked, eyeing the box.

"To keep the secret in," said the woman. "Can't have them flying about the market for all and sundry to take possession of, can we?"

Tourmaline shook her head politely. "My secret is ... it's that I don't know who my father is." She blinked. It wasn't true, of course, but it had been until quite recently. She wasn't sure what had made that particular lie come out of her mouth above all the others she could have told.

The woman's expression turned into an indulgent kind of amused that Tourmaline had seen on very patient and good-tempered adults before. "You can't learn about magic unless you actually make the payment," she said, in a tone that matched her smile.

"Fine," said Tourmaline, completely shameless about being caught in the lie and still hoping that she could get away without telling the woman an *actual* secret.

"My secret is that I don't know how to read a map."

She wondered if that was really good enough. But it was at least a bit true. She'd needed Mai's help more than once trying to find the island of Elsewhere.

The woman looked at the box. Nothing happened.

She tilted her head and sighed. "Well, that's certainly true, but it's also not a secret. Everyone knows you can't read a map."

"Do they?" asked Tourmaline, a little indignantly. She thought she'd done a pretty good job of keeping it hidden.

The woman sighed. "Look, I'm not in the business of forcing people to reveal their secrets, but if you're not going to—"

"No, I am," said Tourmaline quickly. "But are you sure you haven't sent any postcards out to anyone recently?"

The woman looked mystified. "I'm very sure."

Tourmaline bit her lip and thought about George. But she didn't need to tell the woman about her magic.

All she needed was one thing that was true. And if she couldn't tell *one* real secret to a nice woman who had already promised to help and who was the type of adult who worked at a magical market, then she'd never be able to tell anyone and then she'd never get help with her magic.

She looked at the woman's pleasant dimples and thought that anyone who had dimples could probably be trusted. Maybe she could just tell *part* of the secret and not what had happened as a result. "One time I touched the Source," she said, as quickly as she could so it wouldn't be such a big deal to let it out. "The Source of all magic."

"Touched it?" the woman said sharply.

Tourmaline fidgeted in her seat. "Sort of ... fell into it a bit."

The woman's eyes widened and Tourmaline had a very brief but very strong sensation that she maybe shouldn't have told even that part of her biggest, deepest secret.

Chapter Eight

The box suddenly snapped shut and the woman smiled and stood up. "Perfect," she said.

"Oh. Good," said Tourmaline. "Are you going to tell me about magic now?"

The woman opened the tent flap and the riotous noise of the market returned. Tourmaline followed her back out to the barrow and was relieved to see Mai's expectant face and George's anxious one waiting for her.

"Just one minute," said the woman. "Let me confer with a colleague." She walked a short distance away, beckoning to another woman. They put their heads together and began to talk quietly, glancing at the children.

"Did she help?" asked Mai. "Did you find out how

to stop the magic?"

"Not yet," said Tourmaline.

"Is she *going* to help?" asked George, watching the two women anxiously. "What secret did you tell?"

"I think so," said Tourmaline, ignoring George's second question. "I hope so." That didn't exactly cover how much she wanted this to work. She couldn't spend the rest of her life thinking about what the AICMA agents would do with her if they found out. Wondering about it for several weeks had turned out to be extremely wearing and possibly even worse than it just happening.

She sighed wistfully, thinking back to the time when the worst thing she could have been caught doing was liberating a cherry pie from the university kitchens.

"Who's that?" George suddenly looked wary, his brown eyes worried. Mai followed his gaze and caught a glimpse of a shadowy figure hovering on the edge of her vision. She spun round but the figure was gone, swept back into the darkness next to a stall lit with a hazy light that might have been green and might have been purple.

Tourmaline was still staring intently at the red-haired woman and fidgeting from one leg to the other.

Mai spoke to George in a low voice. "Did you see someone too?"

"I thought I did..." George peered into the dark next to the stall, but it was just dark now. Either both of their minds were playing tricks, or there had been somebody there staring at the children. Somebody who hadn't wanted to be seen.

"There you are," said Persephone, suddenly appearing beside them and making them all start. "I distinctly remember asking you to stay close and follow me. Do you know, I just had the most illuminating conversation with one of the vendors. Apparently they have a magical artefact that can detect the presence of anyone from the Agency at a distance of two miles – like a metal detector, only for AICMA agents. Isn't that incredible?"

"Yes," said George loudly.

The red-haired woman was coming back. Tourmaline hastily took her mother by the arm and towed her away. "I'll come back later!" she called over her shoulder to the bemused-looking woman while Mai and George closed in around Persephone.

"Do you know what else I saw at that stall?" said Persephone, sounding like an overeager child at a birthday buffet. "It was the most wonderful magical compass. The vendor said you only have to speak the name of the place you want to go to and it will direct you there—Where are we going now?"

"There are lots of other stalls. Look," said Tourmaline, casting a glance over her shoulder. They walked further round the curve of the market, weaving past someone in a dark cloak who smelled of bitter herbs.

Persephone frowned. "Do you think we should at least try to contact the Agency? I did say that I would—"

"Not before we've seen everything," said Tourmaline quickly. "And what about the magical artefact that you promised to get for the people you borrowed the airship from?"

Persephone was nodding before Tourmaline had finished her sentence. "Maybe it would be best if we made a thorough assessment first, before I send a message to Emiko. And I *do* need to— Oh, would you look at that?" Persephone had noticed a stall like a miniature library, except that some of the books were hovering slightly above the shelves, their pages softly concertinaing. "This looks promising for the university."

The children stood by the shelves as Persephone started asking questions about the books. One with a ship quite like *The Hunter* on the cover tried to nudge Tourmaline into picking it up, so she stuck her hands in her pockets in case she got too tempted. The very last thing they needed was a magical incident with her mother right there and the AICMA only a message in a bottle away.

"You'll have to find a way to go back," said Mai.

"I know," said Tourmaline, who was itching to hear what the red-haired woman had to say.

"Maybe Mai and I could distract Persephone," said George. He said it so easily, Tourmaline was surprised.

"That's not like you," she said. "But thanks."

"I know," said George. "I think I went so much farther than I ever expected I would by hiding in the airship that now I'm not quite sure what I'm capable of."

"Aren't you worried?" Tourmaline asked, with even more surprise.

George thought about it and then said gravely, "I think, considering the amount of trouble I'm in, it's past that now."

Tourmaline nodded. She had often had similar feelings herself but had never expected George to share them.

"Tourmaline?" called Persephone. "I have a very promising lead here. I'm just going to..." She waved her hand in the direction of a tent behind the book stall that might or might not have been there before, but was certainly there now. "Do you think you'll be all right for a moment?"

"Definitely," said Tourmaline cheerfully.

"Stay together," said Persephone.

"We absolutely will," said Mai.

Persephone disappeared into the tent, and Tourmaline smiled. "You've given me an idea, George," she said. She first carefully, and then very quickly, stepped away from the books and the stall and the tent and her mother.

"Are we just going to...?" Mai gestured in the direction of the barrow and the answers.

"Sneak away?" said Tourmaline. "Yes. Yes, we are. I can't think of anything else and I have to do this before we leave, or the Agency get here, or that woman asks for another secret."

They arrived back at the barrow out of breath. But the red-haired woman was nowhere to be seen. Instead, there was a younger girl with dark brown skin and large brown eyes running the stall.

"Where's the other woman?" asked Tourmaline.

"She means, excuse me, where is the other woman, please?" said George.

"Yes, that," said Tourmaline.

"What other woman?" asked the girl. Her face was carefully blank, but her eyes were watchful.

"The one with hair like mine only red," said Tourmaline impatiently. "She was right here and I *need* to see her."

The girl's eyes suddenly got a funny look in them as

she took in Tourmaline's hair and her freckles. "Were you here before?" she asked.

"Yes," said Tourmaline eagerly. "I already told a secret and now I want to know ... I want to know the thing I asked her about."

"Will you wait?" asked the girl. "Right here? And watch the barrow?"

"Yes, but can you be quick?" Tourmaline glanced at George and then back at the girl. "Please?"

The girl ran off, glancing behind her and then running faster.

Tourmaline stared after her and then at her friends.

George looked concerned – which in itself wasn't unusual. Mai was frowning hard.

"Do you think everything's OK?" asked Tourmaline.

"I hope so," said Mai, still frowning. Then she noticed Tourmaline's anxious face trying not to look anxious. "It's going to be fine," she said firmly. "Isn't it, George?"

George looked less sure, but he always looked less sure, so Tourmaline still found it heartening when he nodded hard. "This is what we came for," he said.

"You did what she asked and she said she'd tell you about your magic." He stood on his tiptoes to look for the girl or the red-haired woman returning.

Tourmaline didn't even notice when her hands wandered, fiddled and then picked up something from the barrow that might have been a very small musical instrument. It was round and hollow and had holes in the body of it and in one end.

She put the musical thing to her lips absently and blew, then realized that it was tethered to the stall by a thin piece of cord that strung everything on the barrow together and held them in place. They could be touched but not taken. She was just thinking that it was a very clever way of preventing thievery – and that more people should do that if they didn't want their belongings borrowed – when something that she very much didn't want to happen started happening.

"Oh," said Mai, turning round at the commotion. "Oh no."

George's eyes went wide and his hand flew to his mouth, but it wasn't enough to stop his next, strangled words. "Tourmaline! Your magic!"

Tourmaline stood there, a look of utter shock on her face, her glowing hands held up guiltily in front of her. Something incredible had happened to every single magical artefact on the stall.

Chapter Nine

The light in Tourmaline's hands glowed so brightly in the night air that her face was lit from below. She'd blown one long, eerie note on the musical instrument and all the magical artefacts had been set off like a box of fireworks.

A tray of bright scarab beetle brooches scuttled as far as their tethers would let them, skittering over the stall and the other items. The scenes inside a box of snow globes suddenly came to life, tiny snowdrifts and whirling snowflakes inflicting blizzards on the hapless inhabitants. A collection of hats started constricting and expanding where they hung at the top of the stall, and every whistle and pipe shrilled like a collection of frantic tea kettles. A stack of postcards fluttered in the air, the pictures on them flitting from light to dark and back again.

"Put it down!" said George.

"What?" Tourmaline was panic-stricken.

"The thing you're holding!" said George. "Put it down. They're all joined together!"

Tourmaline realized she was still holding the little instrument and hastily shoved it back on to the stall. She stuffed her hands hurriedly into her pockets, which made absolutely no difference because it was far too late. As she looked back up, she saw that everyone and everything at the market had stopped.

Everyone had seen.

The woman with the red hair had arrived. The girl who'd run off to fetch her was staring, open-mouthed. The woman, however, was smiling, and this time it wasn't exactly friendly. She looked more like Captain Violet did when she had seen something she very much wanted. Like Evelyn Coltsbody when he'd been on the island of Elsewhere. As though Tourmaline herself was the finest of trophies and the red-haired woman had just won first place.

"Tourmaline?" George was wide-eyed. Mai was frozen

in place, blinking at her friends.

Tourmaline took one slow step away from the stall. "I think it's time," she said, "for us to leave." She took George's hand and they started walking away extremely quickly as the market burst back into life again with a series of gasps and a buzz of shocked and excited conversation. "We have to find my mother right away."

The ripple of interest followed them as they ploughed down the corn path.

"That didn't go exactly as planned," said Mai.

"No," said George. "It really didn't." He glanced behind to see several market vendors staring, clearly talking about them. Groups of customers were pointing. They picked up their pace.

"Pssst!" A voice from the tall corn stalks beyond the stalls made George jump.

"Oh no," said Mai. "I'm not dealing with talking plants again."

"It's not a plant," said Tourmaline, pointing between two stalls into the cornfield. A figure was gesturing for them to follow. "This way!" said the voice.

"What do we do?" asked Mai.

Tourmaline looked at the path ahead and then behind. People were starting to gather. It seemed as though they might be thinking about waylaying the children before they could go anywhere.

"Come on," she said, towing George off the path and into the corn.

Mai pushed after them and they dodged through the plants, following the figure. It moved swiftly, leading them a short way through the corn and then back through a quiet part of the market to a darkened tent.

The figure swept the tent flap open, ushered them inside and whipped it closed again.

"We can hide here," they said.

"Who are you?" said Tourmaline.

The person pulled down the hood of their cloak. It was a girl, barely older than Tourmaline, with a pointed elfin face, brown skin and cropped brown hair.

The girl raised her eyebrows and folded her arms. "I just saved you, you know. It wouldn't hurt to say thank you. I saw what you did to Winona's stall."

"So did everybody else," said George to Tourmaline. "We really should leave."

"What about my mother?" said Tourmaline. "Could you take a message to her? Tell her to meet us at the ship?"

"Not until you've paid," said the girl, stepping in front of the tent flap.

"Paid?" said Mai. "For what?"

"For me helping you, of course?"

Tourmaline frowned at the girl. "Thank you for your help," she said, in the same tone of voice she used when she was made to apologize to a professor. "But we don't have any money."

"Oh, never mind all this," said Mai suddenly and she pushed past the girl, reaching for the tent flap.

At that moment, there was a noise outside as though somebody had arrived. Or a lot of somebodies.

Mai cast a look of alarm at her friends and stepped back.

"Tourmaline Grey!" called a familiar voice. "Come outside." It was the red-haired woman – Winona – who Tourmaline had told her secret to. She didn't sound as though she was smiling any more.

Tourmaline glared at the girl in the tent with them.

"How do they know my name?"

The girl raised her eyebrows. "It's not *my* fault. I'm stuck in here with you too, you know. Do you think they're going to be pleased if they realize I was helping you?"

"You *haven't* helped us," said Tourmaline crossly. "And you wanted me to pay you."

"If this is anyone's fault, it's yours," said the girl. "You haven't exactly been careful while you've been here. And did you really think no one was going to find out who you are?"

"Yes," said Tourmaline. "Why would they? I haven't told anyone here my name."

The girl scoffed. "Like you'd have to. You're famous in our world now."

There was a moment of silence.

"Famous?" asked Tourmaline. She sounded both suspicious and quite a bit too pleased.

"Tourmaline, what are we going to do?" said George, in a panicked whisper.

"You're going to come out, because there's nothing else that you can do," called the woman outside the tent.

George looked miserable. Tourmaline squeezed his arm and nodded at Mai.

Mai nodded back with a grim look on her face and opened the tent flap.

But it was the girl who barged out first. "I kept them talking for you, Winona," she said.

"What?" said Tourmaline, very loudly.

The red-haired woman gave the girl a glance that might have been a little suspicious, but she smiled at her. "Well done, Celandine."

Tourmaline had been thinking that it might be best if she and Mai grabbed George and ran, but as they stepped outside, she could see that was impossible. Everyone in the market was there. The girl – Celandine – stood next to Winona. All around Winona were the other vendors, among them the tall man who had sold them chestnuts. There were a lot of adults and none of them looked friendly. George's hand crept into Tourmaline's. These people clearly had no intention of letting the children leave and Tourmaline was sure they had every intention of doing very bad things.

Chapter
Ten

"What do you want?" asked Tourmaline. Her voice only wobbled a bit.

"What could we possibly want with Tourmaline Grey?" asked Winona, smiling round at all the vendors, some of whom laughed. She turned to Tourmaline and the smile was suddenly gone. "The daughter of the famous Persephone Grey, also known to be the daughter of the *in*famous Evelyn Coltsbody – yes, we know about that too – comes to the Dark Market asking about magic and then tells me *she fell into the Source*. And you want to know what we want?"

George's hand suddenly constricted Tourmaline's.

Winona was smiling again, but now it definitely wasn't friendly. "You know where the island of

Elsewhere is, don't you?"

There were so many pairs of eager, greedy eyes on Tourmaline that for once she didn't know what to say.

"That's a yes," said Winona, nudging Celandine with her arm. Celandine's face was unreadable. "So, you can see how valuable you are. A girl who can use magic. Who knows where the Source of all magic is?" She shook her head, as though marvelling at her wonderful luck. "You're the most valuable magical artefact in the whole market."

"Valuable?" Tourmaline wondered if her satchel had become much heavier and was trying to strangle her. "I just wanted to find out about magic," she said. "I don't know where the island is." It was at least partially true. She couldn't have pointed out the spot on a map if her life depended on it. She wondered where her mother was.

"It's true," said Mai. "We don't know anything about ... anything."

"A likely story," said Winona. "First you find the fabled island of Elsewhere and then you come back with your own magic, doing whatever it is you did to my magical artefacts."

"Give over, Winona," said a woman's voice from somewhere in the crowd. "They weren't exactly *all* magical. Some of them are fakes and you know it!"

There were a few raucous laughs that made George jump, even as he frowned at the comment.

"You look a lot like your mother, you know," said Winona. "Which made it easy to find her and have her thrown out of the market."

Tourmaline's hands tightened into fists and George winced.

Winona laughed. "Don't worry, she's fine. We're not interested in her. She won't be able to find her way back into the market, of course. We have ways of seeing to that."

Several people in the crowd chuckled. It made Tourmaline furious.

"Make her tell us where the island is!" a man growled, which reminded Tourmaline that they were very much in danger, that everything was very much worse than it had been before, and that they probably should never have come here in the first place.

"Oh, I will," said Winona, taking a step towards Tourmaline. "We're not letting this one get away."

"You can't have Tourmaline," said Mai, stepping in front of her friend. "She's ours."

"That's right!" said George. He found that even though he wanted to move too, he couldn't, so he settled for nodding hard.

"Maybe she should have thought about that before she blabbed her deepest secret then flaunted her magic all over the place," said Winona.

"I do not blab or flaunt," said Tourmaline indignantly and she let go of George's hand to cross her arms.

Celandine looked at Tourmaline appraisingly and said to Winona, in a very matter-of-fact way, "Are you keeping all three of them?"

"Keeping us?" said Tourmaline, now absolutely outraged. "What do you mean, *keeping* us?" Her neck was getting hot and her arms suddenly felt so strange that she had to shake them a bit to make sure they were still hers.

Winona took another step towards Tourmaline. George found that his legs were braver than he was, and he took a step in front of her on the other side to Mai.

Tourmaline, who had no intention of letting her friends deal with this alone, pushed between them. Winona looked around, gave a tilt of her chin to someone in the crowd and gestured to some other people. "Put them in my tent and seal it."

Mai raised her fists as though she was going to fight. George squeaked as a large woman took hold of him. Then the two of them were pulled away from Tourmaline before Tourmaline herself was manhandled.

"You can't just lock us away," said Tourmaline desperately.

"That's right," said George, although his voice sounded very high. "All the customers will see."

"What customers?" said Winona, opening her hands and looking around. "They all left when the market closed for the night and moved on."

"Moved on?" said Tourmaline, a sudden bolt of panic making her face cold.

It was true. The market was quiet and empty as they were marched back to Winona's barrow and pushed behind it towards the small tent.

Tourmaline was thrown into it, rubbing her arm where

she'd been grabbed. Mai aimed a kick at the man holding her but missed as she stumbled on to the ground.

All sound cut out as soon as the man closed the tent flap, just as it had when Tourmaline had been there before. The table and chairs and the secrets box were gone.

And then the children were alone in the silent tent.

"What are we going to do?" asked Mai. Her voice sounded loud in the silence.

No one answered her. Tourmaline pulled at the tent flaps then kicked at the sides but it seemed as though they were made of iron instead of canvas. Mai tried to pull up the bottom of the tent, then dig into the ground. It was all solid, immoveable.

"That girl Celandine tricked us," said Tourmaline. Her face was mutinous.

"I'm not sure," said George.

"She did know that horrible woman Winona," said Mai, "and she seemed to belong at the market. Maybe she was working with them all along."

George's brow furrowed. "Why didn't she just lead us straight to them, then? And she said she was going to get in trouble for trying to help us."

"Hmm, she did say that," said Mai. "Maybe she *was* trying to help us then she had to lie and pretend she wasn't just to stay out of trouble."

"If that's true," said George, "it's quite clever of her."

"Maybe she's just a big liar who lies," said Tourmaline, who had witnessed these musings with growing annoyance. "Just like everyone else here."

She threw herself down on to the ground, wrenched her satchel off angrily and dug the postcard out from the bottom. It had a few grease marks on it from all the cake and some of the lettering was smeared. "Do you think Winona sent it to make me come here so she could do this to us?" she said.

"Maybe," said George doubtfully. "But how would she have known you were magic?" He frowned. "I mean, before you told her."

Tourmaline looked down at the ground a bit guiltily and then back up at George. She sighed. "I never said I was *magic*. I just said I'd fallen into the Source. I'm really sorry, George. I was desperate and I thought she was going to help me."

There was a quiet moment where they all thought

about poor choices.

"What do you think she's going to do with me?" Tourmaline asked quietly, not at all sure that she wanted to know the answer. There were a few slices of very squashed cake left in the satchel and she handed them out.

"She might want to keep you prisoner forever and do experiments until she finds out what you can do," said Mai. "Or maybe she's going to give you to the AICMA for a reward? Ooh, or there might be rogue hunters like Evelyn Coltsbody who—"

"Yes, all right, never mind," said George quickly.

Tourmaline swallowed her chunk of cake and took another, rather vicious bite.

"Oh!" he said suddenly. "Tourmaline, use your magic!"

Tourmaline stared at him, her mouth full of cake. "What do you mean? I can't— Wait, you mean to try to escape?" She scrambled up on to her knees, looking excited. But the look faded and she didn't move. "I don't know how. That's the whole reason we're here."

"Just try," said George. "You never know when it's going to work, so maybe it's going to work right now."

Tourmaline put her hands on the sealed tent flap. Nothing happened.

She gave it a push. "It's not a magical artefact, George."

"Don't you feel anything?" he asked cautiously.

"I feel terrible," said Tourmaline. "What use is having magic if I can't even do anything with it?"

She slid back down the rigid side of the tent, her boots pushing out on to the flattened corn on the ground.

"Are you going to eat that?" asked Mai. George hadn't touched his cake.

"I don't think I can," said George, but when she reached out for it, he held on to it just in case.

"I thought your worrying had gone since you stowed away," said Mai.

George looked around their prison and at his dejected best friend who didn't know what was going to happen to her.

"It's come back," he said morosely.

Chapter Eleven

Tourmaline woke up. She was still leaning against the side of the tent. She sighed loudly, rubbed her face hard and shuffled around – partly because she was uncomfortable and partly to wake up the others because she didn't want to be alone. By the time she'd finished fidgeting, Mai was blinking at her and George had sat up.

"We're still here," said George quite sadly, as though he had hoped the situation might have remedied itself by now. "What time do you think it is?"

"I don't know," said Tourmaline.

"Do you think they're going to feed us?" asked Mai.

Tourmaline rummaged around in her satchel but there was nothing left except a few sticky crumbs.

She licked her fingers. Then remembered the satchel

had a slim front pocket – unlikely to contain any cake but she might have slid a biscuit in there at some point. She opened it. And stared.

"What?" asked George, immediately looking wary.

Tourmaline wiped her hands on her trousers hastily and pulled out a postcard.

A new one.

Her fingers flared with light for a brief second before it blinked out.

George's eyes widened. He and Mai scrambled to Tourmaline's side. "How did that get there?" he asked. "How *long* has it been there?"

"Someone could have put it there when we were buying chestnuts," said Mai. "Or ... or any time since we arrived!"

"Did your magic change the picture, Tourmaline?" asked George.

"I don't know," she said.

The picture was of a tranquil-looking meadow, a clearing in some woods, the whole scene bathed in warm sunlight.

"Read it!" said Mai. Then, "Wait a minute."

She grabbed Tourmaline's hand before she could turn the card over. "I recognize that picture."

"I've seen it before too," said Tourmaline.

George frowned. "I don't know it. Have you been there?"

"No," said Mai, "but this exact picture is—"

"Hanging in your mother's office!" said Tourmaline.

"In Emiko's office?" said George, looking puzzled. "Are you sure?" His eyes widened. "It can't be her sending them, can it?"

"Of course not," said Mai. "The AICMA don't know about Tourmaline. And none of their agents have ever managed to get near the market."

Tourmaline had already flipped the card and they all leaned forwards to read it.

> Your secret is out,
> But what will you do?
> What you learned at the market,
> Could really help you.
>
> The Museum of Marvels
> can give you the rest, Tourmaline.

Tourmaline scoffed loudly. "What I learned at the market? Well, let's see. I've learned that you can't trust anyone. *Including* whoever is sending these stupid postcards."

She threw it on the floor.

"Whoever it is, they're here at the market," said Mai.

"She's right," said George. "Your secret is out? They must have seen what you did to Winona's stall."

"So whoever it is must have put the postcard in Tourmaline's bag after that," said Mai. "Do you remember anyone getting close to you?"

Tourmaline shrugged.

George picked up the postcard. "Can I have the other one, Tourmaline?"

"You can have them both and set fire to them for all I care," she said, tossing it to him and turning away with her arms folded.

Mai and George exchanged a look. A look that said Tourmaline might need a minute.

"It's the same writing," said George.

"What do you think the Museum of Marvels is?"

asked Mai, her brown eyes shining.

"Who cares?" said Tourmaline loudly.

"It sounds wonderful," said George.

Tourmaline snorted. "So did the Dark Market and look how that's turned out."

"It says what she learned here could really help her," said Mai, ignoring Tourmaline's sulk.

"I didn't learn *anything*," said Tourmaline, determined to sulk for as long as she needed to.

George pondered this for a moment. "I don't think that's true." His face cleared. "Will you try something, Tourmaline? For me?"

Tourmaline had been scowling determinedly at the floor, but after a few seconds she sighed. She couldn't say no to George. "What is it?"

"Do you still have the magical artefact coin? The lucky one?"

Tourmaline snorted so loudly she coughed. "This one?" She took it out of her pocket. "It's definitely not lucky, George."

"Just ... try," said George, taking Tourmaline's free hand and putting it on the tent flap.

Mai pushed up on to her knees. "Do you think it will work?"

"Tourmaline, *please*," said George, and he looked so hopeful that she really did want to try. She pushed against the flap hard but this time she squeezed the coin too. And because she didn't know what else to do, she made a wish, like when you blow birthday candles out.

Please work, she thought at the coin, and *Please let us out* at the tent. Then she closed her eyes, because that worked with birthday candles too, and wished very hard that the coin would change their luck.

"Is anything happening?" asked George. It was a desperate sort of experiment and he wasn't sure that it would work, but much stranger things had happened so he couldn't rule it out.

"The canvas is getting warm," said Tourmaline, and she opened one eye then the other.

"That's probably your hand getting sweaty," said Mai.

"No, it's not," said George, scrabbling over to the sealed flap. "Well, it might be that too, but look!"

The tent flap had come loose.

Tourmaline tugged on it experimentally. It was

126

definitely open. The hope she'd been feeling turned into triumph and amazement that showed on her face as she looked over her shoulder at George and Mai. "It worked," she said. And then, "I thought it would."

She snatched up her satchel and the postcards. "I made it work," she said. "Just like I made the magical artefacts on Winona's stall work."

"Don't forget the postcard," said Mai. "That's a magical artefact too."

"See!" said George. "We *did* learn something."

"Whatever it is I learned, you'll have to tell me later. There's no time now, George," said Tourmaline, entirely her buoyant self again now that they were free. Her hazel eyes were bright and her face was alive with a plan. "Follow me," she said.

"Where are we going?" asked George, cautiously.

"To the Museum of Marvels, of course," said Tourmaline. She smiled. "But we have to make a couple of stops on the way."

Chapter Twelve

Tourmaline stuck her head out of the tent flap. The noise and smells of the market were still there. She ducked back to George and Mai.

"The customers haven't gone at all!" she said. "The market is still right there and it's as busy as ever. Winona lied. She's at the barrow serving customers."

"What a surprise," said Mai, folding her arms and looking unimpressed.

Tourmaline, who had been just the smallest amount of scared, was back into fully outraged mode. "That's it, I've had enough. We're leaving."

"What if she sees us?" said George, his eyebrows at maximum worry.

"What if she comes back in and we're still here?"

said Tourmaline. She slipped out into the night, Mai following. George took a deep breath, told himself that Tourmaline was right and quietly eased through the tent flap.

They edged around the tent in the shadows until they reached the line of corn behind it.

"George," said Tourmaline very quietly. "Remember to breathe."

George nodded. They stepped just inside the corn and followed it along the edge of the market until Tourmaline put a hand up to stop them. She pointed at a stall that sold clothes – striped jumpers and jackets with shiny buttons, hats with feathers, and cloaks, capes and tall boots.

"The airship is that way," George whispered.

"I know," said Tourmaline. She was about to tell George something he wouldn't want to hear, so she squeezed his hand. "We have to go back into the market, just for a minute."

George's face said *what for?* and *Tourmaline, no* and *can't we just leave?*

Tourmaline looked at him sympathetically. "We have

to get the compass my mother mentioned."

George shook his head. "But—"

"How are we going to find the Museum of Marvels without it?" asked Tourmaline. "Or get home? And what about my mother? It might be able to find her too."

George blinked. He didn't have any answer to that.

"So why have we stopped here?" asked Mai, frowning at the clothing stall. "This isn't where the compass— Oh!" She paused, a look of excitement on her face. "Disguises?"

Tourmaline nodded. "We can't go back in like this. But if we don't look like ourselves, no one will take any notice."

She glanced at George to see if all this was having the desired persuading effect. "We have to hurry, before anyone notices that we've escaped."

George had several misgivings but the children were so close to the vendor he didn't dare voice them. He nodded instead.

Tourmaline gave his hand an extra squeeze. "Stay here. I've got a plan."

The stalls were all busy, the vendors having returned to a brisk trade while the children had been locked up. The sky was starting to lighten from midnight black to a deep purple. Tourmaline wondered what would happen to the market once the sun came up, but she didn't intend to be here to find out.

She crouched down and crawled through the corn and right past the vendor's legs until she was under the stall. From there, she reached up, snagged a handful of material from the far end of the table and whipped it down. George had to turn away, the stress of watching entirely too much for him. This was bold, even for Tourmaline.

But she had a plan, and when Tourmaline had a plan, there was no stopping her. She pulled another handful of clothes down and then made her way back through the corn to dump them breathlessly and triumphantly at Mai and George's feet.

They retreated further back into the corn before they started pulling on the clothes. George picked up a cloak, tried it on and discarded it since it was much too long.

"Maybe we should have left a coin behind," he said

quietly. "Or an IOU note or something."

Tourmaline stared at her friend incredulously. "They *kidnapped* us, George. That's worse than borrowing some clothes."

"Just because they did something bad, it doesn't make it OK for us to do bad things too," he said.

Tourmaline, who always tried to be patient with George's qualms even when she didn't feel them herself, sighed. "We'll leave the clothes on the ground at the edge of the cornfield after we've escaped with the compass, OK?"

George smiled. "Thanks, Tourmaline." He pulled on a large, striped jumper and tugged a large floppy hat into place. "Whoever sent the postcard was right, you know," he said. "We did learn something that can help us figure out your magic."

"I haven't had much time to think about it," said Tourmaline. She pulled a feathered hat all the way down over her hair and tucked a few stray curls under it.

"The magic in our world," said George, more thoughtfully now, "is wearing out. Just look at the Archives at Pellavere. It's unpredictable and it isn't working properly. The postcard didn't work for me either. But it did work for you. You made it ... *more*."

"I make magical artefacts more?" said Tourmaline uncertainly.

"That does make sense," said Mai. She picked up the cloak that George had discarded and swept it around her shoulders. "Tourmaline is extra."

George nodded eagerly, pleased that he had finally worked out what Tourmaline's magic was. "We already knew about the rope-ness of the rope and the cat-ness of Fitzsimmons, and now we know about—"

"The Tourmaline-ness of Tourmaline," Mai finished.

"You amplify magical artefacts," said George triumphantly. "You can make magical artefacts work properly again. Maybe even better than they did before. That's what happened on the stall in the market when you set them all off. And with the coin in the tent."

Tourmaline frowned. It didn't explain the fiasco with the sinks back at the university. Or the incident in the science lab. The taps hadn't been magical artefacts. Neither had the Bunsen burner, unless she was very much mistaken.

But maybe George was right and the magic was unpredictable because it was wearing out.

George's eyebrows took on a slight tilt. "So it *was* worth coming here after all. Aren't you happy to know what you can do?"

"Of course I am, George. Really. It's just that I still don't know how to stop it happening. And people will still want to lock me up or do experiments or whatever if they find out. The postcard sender might have been right about coming here, but they weren't here to meet me like they said they would be."

"Maybe they were," said Mai, "but then the whole thing with Winona's stall happened."

Tourmaline surveyed her friends. "Either way, we don't have time for this now. We have a compass to steal."

"Yes, we do," said Mai. She looked entirely too pleased for George's liking. "Imagine a magical artefact that can show you the way to anywhere you want to go if you just ask it."

Mai pulled up the hood on her cloak and then examined Tourmaline's costume, tugging her friend's hat down for her and poking at a curl that had escaped.

"The compass is on the stall next to the chestnut cart, which is pretty close to where we came into the market," said Tourmaline. "All we have to do is take it and leave. OK?"

"I like the part about leaving," said George. "We need to be extra careful and not just because of Winona. The postcard sender is out there somewhere and they might have been at least partly right about coming here, but we still don't know what they want."

"What about Persephone?" asked Mai.

"If she's not back at the ship, we can look for her when we're in the air," said Tourmaline. "Now, let's go. George, are you ready to go out there?"

George secured his floppy hat, told himself that this was all to help Tourmaline, and nodded.

They pushed through the corn and slipped back into the market.

"Don't walk too fast," said Mai, pulling George back. "It might seem suspicious."

George looked worried and slowed to a dawdle, so Tourmaline linked his arm in hers. She ducked her head, hoped no one had realized that they had escaped and towed him along, looking for the right stall.

There were still plenty of other customers, some with hoods pulled low over their faces, others with bags and baskets bulging with items. One man wandered past with a collection of musical instruments all jangling out of time and another woman had a huge lizard wearing a harness and a leash.

When they reached the right place, the stall was busy. They stood back in the shadows. George kept his head so far down he couldn't actually see anything other than the ground. Mai stood first on one leg and then the other.

"Come on," she said, pulling at Tourmaline's arm. "George, will you be lookout?"

George seemed torn over which would be worse – going over to the stall or staying behind on his own – but Tourmaline had already gone.

Several other customers were browsing the goods and one was engaged in some complicated haggling over a pendant necklace that the vendor said was guaranteed to make the wearer seventeen per cent more beautiful.

Tourmaline's eyes roved across the items laid out. They each had a small cream name card in front of them with a description of what they did. She saw a knife that never needed sharpening and a set of knitting needles that never dropped a stitch, but no compass.

"Where is it?" hissed Mai.

George was peering over at the stall and tugging nervously on the cuffs of his jumper. There was a pile of coloured thread at his feet.

"I don't know," Tourmaline hissed back. "It should be here but it's not."

At that moment, Tourmaline felt a strange sensation on the top of her head. It was such an odd tingling that she nudged Mai. But Tourmaline wasn't the only one who had noticed something strange happening.

"I've never seen one of those hats do that before," said the vendor, looking at Tourmaline with curious, narrowed eyes.

"What's it doing?" asked Tourmaline. Her eyes were wide and even her *hair* was starting to feel unusual.

"It looks like it's trying to ... eat your hair," said Mai.

Tourmaline reached up to pull the hat off. It dodged

out of the way, spilling out some of her hair.

She gasped and pulled harder. Everyone was looking at her.

Mai took her by the arm and pulled hard. "Perhaps we'd better come back later," she said.

As they charged away from the stall, and the hat finally came free, George gawked. "Tourmaline, what's happened to your hair?"

Tourmaline's curls had all straightened. Her hair hung six inches longer than it had before and she didn't look like herself at all.

She touched it, feeling and looking startled. "I don't want straight hair," she said. "I have *curls*."

"The hat must be a magical artefact," said George. "Maybe the chestnut man was lying about the clothes being non-magical. Also? I really think we should leave right now."

"But what about the compass?" said Tourmaline. "I can't go back to pretending I'm not magic now. I have to follow the postcards. I *have* to go to the museum."

"I don't like the way they're looking at us," said Mai quietly. She tilted her head back at the customers and vendor at the stall. The children all took a few hurried steps away and ducked into the darkness between two tents.

"If the compass is gone," said Tourmaline, "we have to find something else that can help."

"Tourmaline." The voice came sudden and quiet, next to her ear.

She spun round to see a figure in the darkness.

Chapter Thirteen

"You!" said Tourmaline, a scowl already halfway across her face.

It was the girl – the probably untrustworthy one – Celandine. From behind her, someone else stepped out. Someone a lot more trustworthy.

"Oh!" said Tourmaline.

"Persephone!" said George.

Persephone smiled a relieved smile at George and Mai and took hold of Tourmaline's hands.

"Thank goodness I found you," she said. "Are you all OK? What are you wearing? And Tourmaline, what happened to your hair? Not that it isn't lovely. But— Oh, never mind that. I thought you were locked up. What did they do to you, and *why*?"

Tourmaline gave Celandine a look. Evidently, she hadn't told Persephone the reason Tourmaline had been captured, but Tourmaline wasn't sure why. She pawed at her strangely smooth and floppy hair. "It's a bit of a magical mistake," she said, stuffing the offending hat into a pocket so it couldn't do anything else.

"I helped Persephone get back into the market," said Celandine. "You're welcome, by the way."

Tourmaline gave her a half-scowl as a compromise since she still wasn't at all sure she could trust the girl.

"That's right," said Persephone. "I had a very confusing and frustrating time wandering around a cornfield, completely unable to find my way back in for reasons I suspect were magical in some way. And then this rather intrepid and wonderful young woman found me and helped me sneak back in." She smiled entirely too kindly at Celandine for Tourmaline's liking. "And now we're here to rescue you. But it seems that you rescued yourselves instead. Should we leave?"

"Immediately," said George. He turned to back out on to the main thoroughfare of the market and made a noise. An anguished squeak. "Oh no, not again."

"Terribly sorry," said the tall man from the chestnut stall. He was blocking the gap between the two tents. "But you really are very valuable."

"There are people behind you, so don't bother running into the corn," said Winona, stepping up next to the man. "Celandine, is that you?" Her face took on an expression of deep suspicion.

"Are these the people that locked you up?" said Persephone. She sounded like a protective mother and therefore very dangerous.

"In a tent," said George. "With no food."

"No food?" Persephone sounded outraged. "Well, we can't have that." Quick as a flash (which turned out to be very appropriate), she pulled something from her pocket and held it up at arm's length in front of herself. A blinding light appeared.

Tourmaline shielded her eyes. The light intensified into a great flash then was gone. She blinked the black spots out of her eyes and saw that her mother was holding out a large camera with a leather strap and a round lens cover dangling from it. Winona and the tall man appeared to be transfixed by the flash, as still as if the photograph had frozen them in time. But the most alarming thing about the whole scene was that they were both – from head to foot – grey.

There was a second of stunned silence.

"What have you done to them?" asked George.

"Nothing so very bad," said Persephone. "And nothing so very permanent either."

"Why are they all grey, then?" asked Tourmaline.

"It's black-and-white film in the camera," said Persephone, as though that were perfectly logical. "It will wear off. Eventually. Or so I'm told."

"It's a magical artefact!" said Mai.

"Yes, I picked up a couple of things. Thought they might come in handy," said Persephone cheerfully. "Tourmaline, I'm rescuing you." She sounded quite pleased about it. "What's the matter?"

Tourmaline was not so pleased. No self-respecting hunter/adventurer got rescued by their mother.

Persephone seemed to read Tourmaline's mind. She gave Tourmaline a very motherly look – mildly disapproving but loving. And then she said, "It's OK to need help sometimes. And to accept it. You don't have to do *everything* yourself. Now, before you go anywhere, is someone going to explain to me why these people locked my daughter up and why this awful man just described her as 'valuable'?"

Tourmaline looked at George and then at Mai and then at Celandine and then at the ground. "I ... I'm magic now. Since I fell into the Source."

She risked a quick glance at her mother's face to see how bad it was.

Persephone looked very surprised, then worried, then full of some other feelings that might have been protective and proud. Then she spoke. "I wish you had told me, Tourmaline. I think I understand why you didn't, but I really wish you had."

Tourmaline looked at her mother anxiously. "I didn't want you to worry."

"It's in my job description as your mother," said Persephone. "Is this why you wanted to come here so badly?"

Tourmaline nodded miserably. "I needed to learn about ... me."

"Here's what I think about you," said Persephone.

"You are mine and I love every part of you. And if this is part of you, Tourmaline, then I love it too. I don't want you to have to hide anything about yourself. Not from me, and not from anyone else."

Tourmaline's eyes got quite watery and she had to blink a lot before she could speak. "But what about the – the tent and the kidnapping? And what if the Agency wants to lock me away too?"

"There'll be no more of that," said Persephone fiercely. She brandished the camera. "Now tell me, Tourmaline. What do you need?"

"Need? I..." Tourmaline looked at her friends, who both nodded their encouragement. "I need to go to the Museum of Marvels. I got a postcard and it said someone knew I was magic and I should come here to the Dark Market if I wanted to learn the truth. So I came and I *did* learn some things. Now I know that I can make magical artefacts *more*—"

"Amplify them," George added.

"But I still don't know how to control it. Then I got another postcard that said I could find out how if I went to the Museum of Marvels."

145

She finished and held her breath.

"Well, then," said Persephone. "You have to go."

Just at that moment, Winona's fingers twitched.

George grabbed Tourmaline's arm.

"I think," said Persephone, "that you had better hurry."

"I agree," said Celandine.

Tourmaline glared at her before turning back to her mother. "But what about you?" she asked. "Aren't you coming?"

Persephone had a wary eye firmly on Winona. "I think this is an adventure you can handle by yourself, don't you? Besides, someone needs to hold this button down for a little while longer until you get away." She tilted her head at the camera.

"But I can't leave you," said Tourmaline. "Then *you'll* need rescuing."

"They don't want me," said Persephone. "They want you. And for good reason. You were magical before and now you're even more magical. Anyway, if I mention that the AICMA are on their way, I suspect the market will disappear in no time."

Tourmaline wavered.

Persephone shook her head. "It's not your job to look after me, Tourmaline. It's the other way round."

"I think it's both," said Tourmaline.

"You might be right," said Persephone. "But at the moment it's my turn. Now, go, and hurry. I'll be quite all right. I'll wait here for the AICMA agents."

Tourmaline turned reluctantly to leave.

"Wait!" Persephone dug around in another of her pockets and pulled out something round and shiny, about the size of Tourmaline's palm.

"The compass!" Tourmaline almost laughed.

"I got it for myself, but I think you might need it more."

"Come *on*, Tourmaline," said Mai, edging around Persephone then Winona and backing away down the path.

The grey tinge was starting to seep out of Winona and the chestnut man, colour returning to their clothes first.

"When you've done what you need to do, use the compass to come home and tell me all about your adventure," said Persephone. The way she was looking at Winona, Tourmaline wondered if she should be more worried about the other woman than she was about her mother.

Tourmaline took the compass and kissed Persephone's cheek.

Winona broke free with a roar that startled them all.

Celandine and Mai took off running. George tugged Tourmaline's arm hard and she turned tail and ran.

Chapter Fourteen

Tourmaline's satchel bounced off her back as the children ran, faster than they had ever run before. They hit the wall of corn and blundered through it, thrashing stalks out of the way until the airship was in sight.

Mai jabbed her finger in the direction of the balloon that was bobbing gently in the sky, and they fled towards it, flinging open the doors and throwing themselves inside.

"Up!" George gasped.

"Stop!" said Tourmaline. "What about *her*? We can't take her with us."

Celandine was just as out of breath as the rest of them, but she managed to look pleadingly at George.

"We don't have time for this, Tourmaline," said George firmly. "We have to get you away from the market."

Celandine smiled, Tourmaline scowled and George closed the doors. Mai ran to the controls and threw a lever, then the airship shot up past the top of the tallest tree in the surrounding fields.

"Mai?" said Tourmaline. "Do you think you can fly this ship?"

"Yes," said Mai. "Probably."

"Can you fly over the market to check on my mother?"

They all stood at the front of the ship as Mai piloted it forwards until they came to the place where the market had been.

Instead of the market, there was simply a huge concentric circle of flattened corn. Not a tent or stall, vendor or customer, magical artefact or trinket in sight. The Dark Market had moved on.

They all stared at the scene below for several seconds.

"I'm sure she's all right," said Mai. "She's Persephone."

They scoured the field, looking for a sign.

"I wonder what the farmer is going to think when she sees her field," said George.

"Not that a magical market was there and then suddenly disappeared," said Mai.

"No," said George. "Not that."

There was movement in the corn outside the circle and suddenly Persephone burst through, waving frantically.

Tourmaline sighed a big sigh of relief.

"Does she want us to pick her up?" asked George.

Tourmaline leaned forwards, her nose almost touching the glass. "No, she wants us to..."

Persephone's gestures got wilder.

"Leave," said Tourmaline. "I think the AICMA are on their way."

"Oh dear," said George. "Oh no. We can't let them find..." He looked at Tourmaline, then at the compass in her hand and then at the airship around them. "We can't let them find any of this!"

Tourmaline waved back wildly at her mother, pointing onwards, though she had no idea where they were going.

"Go!" said George.

Mai pulled the lever again, then took the wheel, and the airship shot forwards, past the whole forest, leaving behind the site where the Dark Market had been.

A sparkling lake, shining darkly in the moonlight, came into view. Mai piloted the airship until it was hovering over the middle of the lake – just to make absolutely sure they couldn't be reached by anyone – then pulled the lever, stopped the ship, took a very deep breath and turned to face the others.

"Well done," said Tourmaline.

"Thank you," said Mai, and she sat down very suddenly.

"Are we going to the Museum of Marvels now?" Celandine had been quiet until then but now her brown eyes were bright as they met Tourmaline's.

"*We* are," said Tourmaline, glancing at Mai and George. She crossed her arms.

Celandine crossed her arms right back. "Well, the market's moved on and I'm not exactly welcome there any more thanks to you. So what else am I supposed to do?"

"She does know about the magical world," said Mai.

Tourmaline scoffed.

"Do you know about the museum, then?" asked George.

"Or where it is?" asked Mai.

"We don't need her," said Tourmaline. "We have the compass."

"But *do* you know?" George asked Celandine again, casting a guilty glance at Tourmaline.

Celandine's small, pointed chin scrunched up stubbornly. "Not exactly," she said. "But I know more about magic than any of you."

"We can't trust her. She wanted us to pay her for her help!" said Tourmaline.

Celandine sighed and looked at the floor. "I *tried* to help you escape from Winona because I know what she's like and I felt sorry for you, OK? I was trying to be *nice*. It's not my fault you got caught. And then I *had* to pretend I was on her side. But that's all over now, anyway, since I helped Persephone get back into the market *as well*. I'll never be able to go there again and all because I wanted to do the right thing. The least you could do is say thank you."

"Thank you," said George in a quiet voice.

Celandine gave him a small nod. "Look, I don't have anywhere else to go right now. Can I come with you? It won't be for long. Just until I can get a message to my mother to pick me up." She looked at Tourmaline. "I helped you get back to *your* mother."

Mai looked at Tourmaline. "I don't think it would hurt," she said. "And she did get Persephone back in. If she hadn't, we wouldn't have the compass in the first place, so we wouldn't be able to get to the museum."

There was a brief but fierce exchange of glances between the three friends.

"Oh, all right," said Tourmaline, not very graciously.

She held up the compass. It was as big as her palm, the body of it giving off a dull golden gleam. Around the circumference were many black markings and numerals. Several tiny moving parts and cogs covered its surface.

Tourmaline thought it very impressive. She wasn't sure exactly how it worked but she was very much looking forward to finding out.

"What did Persephone say about how it works?" asked Mai.

"She said you only have to speak the name of the place you want to go to and it will show you the way," said Tourmaline.

She cleared her throat. "Museum of Marvels. Please."

"Is anything happening?" asked Mai.

"My palm is getting very warm," said Tourmaline.

"The same kind of warm as the lucky coin?" asked George, moving back slightly.

"Yes, that kind of warm," said Tourmaline. "And it started when I said Museum of Marvels."

As Tourmaline said the words again, the compass started spinning, the little cogs, dials and levers shifting like a clockwork toy and arranging themselves in new ways. Suddenly the whole top part of the compass lifted open like a pocket watch. Underneath was a miniature map.

George, Mai and Celandine crowded round. They all stared.

Mai let out a startled laugh. "It's moving!"

Tiny waves topped with white froth were lapping against tiny countries. Between the little upright parts of the compass, miniscule clouds flitted across the sky, casting shadows on dotted islands.

As they watched, the smallest airship blinked into view over a smudge of a lake.

"It's us," said George, in absolute wonder. The finest of silver threads tracked its way across Escea to the southern coast and stopped with a pinprick of a star, which then pulsed with light.

Tourmaline looked up at her friends, her eyes wide and intent. "It's working! It's showing us the way to the museum!"

"It's on the other side of Escea," said Mai, frowning over the tiny dot of the museum. Right next to it, the line of the coast tracked down the map, blue sea swelling, miniscule waves cresting.

"Mm," said Tourmaline, though in truth she hadn't a clue what she was looking at.

"I think I can get us there," said Mai.

"I know you can," said Tourmaline, smiling at her friend. She balanced the compass in front of Mai and the airship glided off over Escea.

George yawned widely. It had been a long night with a lot of thoughts. Being scared half to death was very wearing. He looked longingly at the bunk beds behind him, lining the walls of the airship.

Tourmaline put her hands in her pockets and surveyed the wide world as they scudded over it. This was what she had always wanted. This was the feeling that she'd had when they'd set sail on *The Hunter* and the sea air had been in her face and the open ocean had been ahead of her. But now, it wasn't the captain and her crew controlling the vessel and navigating the way. It was Tourmaline herself and her two best friends, even if Celandine was there too. The adventure that lay ahead of them filled her with the most delicious mix of excitement and trepidation and hope and worry.

What if she couldn't find a way to fix her magic and she had to live in a cave on a deserted mountaintop for the rest of her life to stop other people from putting her in a science lab?

What if the answer was right there in the museum like the mystery postcard sender said it was?

"Tourmaline?" George was looking at her with concern. "Are you OK?"

"I think so," she said. "I think we're doing the best thing we can now."

George smiled bravely and hoped with all his heart that his friend was right.

Celandine and Mai were standing at the controls, their heads close together, and talking in low voices when Tourmaline woke up from a nap she hadn't meant to take. She was lying on one of the bunks. George was asleep on the opposite side of the ship. The striped jumper that he had forgotten to return was pulled over his hands, though he'd lost the floppy hat somewhere.

Tourmaline frowned at the back of Mai's head, which looked as though it was enjoying the conversation with Celandine. She scrambled up, pulled her rucked shirt straight and realized that her own head felt a lot more normal.

Mai turned around. "Your curls have come back!"

Tourmaline patted her head and sighed in relief. At least that hadn't been permanent magic.

Mai looked down at a river sparkling in the early

morning sun and made an adjustment to a brass dial on the controls.

"Are we nearly—?" Tourmaline didn't get to finish her question, because Mai suddenly pulled down a large lever and the ship came to a halt. Tourmaline took a step forwards and Mai pointed ahead of them. The view showed an empty clearing in the dawn light.

"This is it!" said Tourmaline. "The exact picture from—" She glanced at Celandine. "From the painting in your mother's office," she finished. She still had deep suspicions about Celandine and no intention of bringing up the postcards in front of her again.

"It's definitely the right place," said Mai, sounding pleased with herself. She frowned. "I wonder why my mother has a painting of it?"

Tourmaline snapped the compass shut and dropped it into one of her pockets. George wandered over with his hair sticking up and yawned widely.

Celandine turned to Tourmaline with a quizzical frown. "Where's the museum? There's nothing here."

"Oh," said Tourmaline. She hadn't thought of that. But Celandine (annoyingly) was right.

"It must be ... behind those trees," said Tourmaline.

Mai nudged the ship forwards. Beyond the clearing and the trees there was a cliff that dropped to the crashing waves of the ocean glinting below.

"It might be an underground museum, like the cavern on the island of Elsewhere," said Mai. "Or maybe it's—" She craned her neck to look up through the window of the airship. "No, it's not up there. Well, maybe it's..."

But Mai didn't have a third option, which was enough to make Tourmaline even more worried than she was already. She took the compass out again and said, "Museum of Marvels."

The compass opened to show a miniature replica of the exact scene they were looking down on. The dot of light that marked the destination glowed right under the tiny airship.

"Do you have any other magical artefacts in here?" asked Celandine. "Maybe we need something else."

When Tourmaline looked over at her, the other girl was rummaging in her satchel.

"That's mine!" said Tourmaline. She rushed over but not before Celandine had pulled out the postcards.

Tourmaline snatched them back.

"Sorry," said Celandine, not looking particularly sorry. "Is that a picture of where we are right now?"

"They're magical postcards," said Mai. "We don't know who sent them but they've been giving us clues about where to go to help Tourmaline with her magic. She touched the first one and it showed her a picture of the Dark Market."

"Mai!" said Tourmaline.

"She might be able to help," said Mai, completely unashamed.

"You don't know how to use your magic?" said Celandine.

"Of course I do," said Tourmaline.

George raised his eyebrows.

"Well, not entirely," said Tourmaline grudgingly. "Not really. No."

"George has a theory that she amplifies magical artefacts," said Mai.

"Because the magic in our world is puttering out," said George. "But Tourmaline can make it strong again. You saw what she did at the market."

Celandine nodded to the postcards. "So what about the second postcard? If you touched the first one and it showed you the Dark Market, then if you touch—"

"The second one it will show me a picture of the Museum of Marvels. I was just about to say that," said Tourmaline.

She was already crouching down, placing the postcards on the floor and running a finger over the latest one.

"You probably have to concentrate quite hard," said George. He patted Tourmaline's shoulder. George was a lot better than she was at concentrating and Tourmaline hoped it might rub off on her.

She put her hand flat on the postcard, closed her eyes and tried to feel the right amount of determined to make the magic work.

"I told you so!" said Celandine.

Tourmaline scowled up at the other girl, then turned her attention to the postcard under her glowing hand. It now showed a large, imposing castle of a building, right there in the previously empty clearing.

Chapter Fifteen

Celandine grinned a mischievous pixie grin.

"The museum is there all right – it's just hidden."

"What do you mean, hidden?" asked George.

"Do you mean with magic?" Mai asked, leaning so far forwards that her nose touched the window. She was looking down on a forest, in the centre of which was a very large clearing. It looked completely uninteresting and very, very empty. Except that if the postcard – and Celandine – were right, it was the complete opposite.

"An invisible museum?" said George frowning. He looked dubious as he pulled down his sleeve and wiped away the smudge Mai's nose had left on the window.

Tourmaline found that she was 1) extremely interested in a magical artefact that could hide a whole building and 2) just as intrigued about what was *inside* the building if it kept its entire self a hidden secret.

"I'll land the ship," said Mai.

"Wait a minute," said George. "I'm not sure I like this."

"Why not?" asked Tourmaline.

Everyone looked at him and he tucked his chin back and stuffed his hands into his pockets. "Why would a museum need to stay hidden?"

Tourmaline shrugged. "To keep it safe from Captain Violet? You don't have to come if you don't want to, George." There hadn't been much time for George to recover from all the adventuring he'd been forced into on Elsewhere. She wondered if defying his mother and stowing away to come on *this* adventure had pushed George to his adventure limit.

She patted his arm and several loose threads fell off his stolen jumper. "Do you want to stay here and guard the ship?" She looked at Celandine. "You can keep her with you."

Celandine looked indignant. "I'm not staying here."

George stood up straighter. "Of course I want to come with you, Tourmaline. It's just that after what happened at the Dark Market, I think we should be very careful. We don't know what, or who, is in there. But a mission like this calls for someone with previous experience. And you didn't make it to the centre of the island of Elsewhere by yourself."

Tourmaline smiled a small, grateful smile. "No, I didn't."

"And me. I helped," said Mai. "In fact, I rescued you."

"Very bravely," said Tourmaline.

"Just land right at the edge of the clearing," said George. "So we don't hit the museum, wherever it is."

He stepped to the front of the ship to fully supervise Mai not hitting something that she couldn't see.

Celandine considered them, her head tilted. "You have very good friends," she said.

"I know," said Tourmaline, and she felt pride burst in her chest.

"Lucky," said Celandine, the look on her face wistful.

Tourmaline studied her more carefully. "Yes, I am."

And with that, the ship bumped down on the ground.

"Let's go," said Tourmaline.

A minute later, with jumpers, satchel and postcards in place, four children stood at the edge of the clearing, looking out into the eerily quiet space.

"How are we supposed to get into the museum if we can't even see it?" asked Mai.

There was a moment of uncertain silence. Then Tourmaline decided that was quite enough of that, and marched out, ignoring George's little "ooh" of caution.

"What are we supposed to do?" asked Mai.

"I'm not exactly sure," said Tourmaline, though she was striding forwards into the long grass with the utmost confidence.

She walked smack into something tall and solid.

As she held her breath and rubbed her knee, George and Mai both made surprised noises. And when Tourmaline herself looked up, she almost forgot what would undoubtedly turn into a large bruise on her leg.

In front of her, a wall shimmered into existence, rising past the height of the surrounding trees. The wall was rough, handmade, ancient-looking. Distinctly and impressively castle-ish.

"Just like the picture on the postcard," said Celandine.

Tourmaline looked up. "I wasn't expecting it to be so..."

"Monstrously big?" George supplied helpfully.

"Yes. That," said Tourmaline.

The rest of the building appeared like a mirage, then solidified into something a lot more fortress-like than anyone had hoped for.

"How are we supposed to get in?" asked Mai, looking to Tourmaline.

"There must be a way," said Tourmaline. "Come on." And she marched off again, along the length of the wall and then round a corner.

The others looked at each other, then hurried after her.

"I think this is the front," Tourmaline called to them. There were several portcullis gates, all small – person-sized to be exact – in a row along the wall. Each one had a neatly engraved brass plaque with a bell pull next to it.

"Administrative," George read out from the first one.

Tourmaline pulled a face in response. "Containment."

"Really?" asked Celandine. She ran over to see.

"What does that even mean?" asked George, slowly and suspiciously.

"I don't know," said Tourmaline, "but I don't think we want it."

"Management," said Mai, having moved along to the third gate.

Tourmaline ran to the next one, glanced at the plaque, then turned to the others, a look of triumph on her face.

"The Museum of Marvels!" she said, and George and Mai hurried to the portcullis where she was standing.

Tourmaline looked at the plaque, her heart aflutter. All museums were marvellous, including the one at Pellavere, but this one was actually, specifically marvellous. Even though it was forbidding and the portcullis was quite alarming, it was still exciting.

The only problem was. how were they going to get in?

George was frowning at the bell pull in front of him when Tourmaline reached out and pulled it, very firmly.

"Tourmaline!" he said, in a scandalized whisper.

"How else are we going to get in?" said Tourmaline, undeterred. "It's not like they're expecting us. The whole place is hidden. And there's probably no one here, anyway – it's very early. So it's definitely worth trying, because if we didn't and then this was the way in—"

There was a rattling sound from deep within the wall. Tourmaline stopped talking. George took his usual step back.

"It's opening," said Mai, pointing as the portcullis jerked up and the rattling sound continued. "Celandine, are you coming?" The girl was still standing by the Containment door.

"Lovely," said Tourmaline, as though she wasn't even the tiniest bit flustered (which she had been since she'd impulsively yanked the bell pull). "Hurry up, then." She ducked under the rising gate and into the dark recess beyond. Mai followed and then Celandine, who had somehow got in front of George.

Crammed into the small space, Tourmaline came face to face with a much more ordinary door. It didn't look in the slightest bit ancient and when she tried it, she found it was locked.

Just as she turned round to report this to the others, the portcullis started lowering again. George, who was partway through it, squeaked and lurched forwards into Celandine, then Mai, who bumped into Tourmaline just as the portcullis hit the ground with a very final-sounding crunch.

"Oh," said Tourmaline. She tried the door in front of her again, giving the knob a good rattle.

George turned round in a circle. There was no bell pull on this side.

"We're trapped!" said Mai.

Chapter
Sixteen

"We can't be trapped," said Tourmaline. She wasn't prone to panic but she was starting to feel as though all this had been a terrible idea.

"What kind of museum does this to people?" asked Mai.

"Maybe we're just here too early and they're not open yet," said Celandine.

"I don't want to be stuck here until someone finds us," said Tourmaline.

"We're fine," said George, causing the three girls to stare at him.

He pointed down to the lower quarter of the door, which was actually a dog (or large cat) flap. Then, to Tourmaline's surprise, he kneeled down, stuck his head through and crawled right in.

"Are you sure," Mai said quietly, "that you pulled the right George out of that mirror on the island?"

"What?" asked Celandine.

"I'll tell you later," said Mai.

"No," said Tourmaline, "you won't. The island is a secret."

"Is she always like this?" Celandine asked Mai.

Tourmaline frowned, so Mai didn't answer. She ducked to follow George, squeezing through more slowly than he had because she was bigger and had to wriggle more. Tourmaline followed, Celandine came last, and they all stood up inside the Museum of Marvels.

Tourmaline stared. And blinked. And stared some more.

"Oh," she said. She said it very quietly (for Tourmaline) and her voice echoed very quietly.

In front of her was a vast, orderly museum, each exhibit neatly labelled and encased in glass, each line of glass cases stretching off into the distance. The roof was a great arc of stone and the aisles were dimly lit.

It was completely silent.

"So many artefacts," said George, his eyes huge and round. "How did they all get here? Are they all magical?"

"Of course they are," said Tourmaline, though she could hardly believe it herself.

"Whoever owns this museum must have been collecting them for years," said Mai in a hushed, library tone of voice.

"Imagine what the world would be like if all these magical artefacts were just *out there*," said George, as though he couldn't decide if that would be wonderful or terrible.

"Why are we the only ones here?" asked Mai.

"Maybe because it's early," said Celandine, looking round cautiously. "Whoever works here hasn't arrived yet. But that just means we get to look round first."

"Right," said Tourmaline, giving herself a little shake. "Come on, then. There must be something here that can tell us all about magic. Or teach me how to stop it. That's what the postcard said, isn't it? So we have to start searching."

George blinked as though he were coming out of a daze.

"What exactly are we looking for?" asked Celandine.

"I'm not sure," said Tourmaline, still suspicious of the other girl. She had made friends with Mai after being uncertain about her, but she wasn't sure if she was ready to be friends with Celandine yet. Maybe she already had enough friends. "A book, maybe? Something that can tell me about magic."

They hurried past a glass case full of clockwork toys. Under any other circumstances, George would have loved to examine them in great detail, especially the small submarine and a rather mystifying snowman. Given that each one was an artefact that had some special, magical use, he was dying to marvel over them. But there was no time for that now.

Next was a series of pens, all busily engaged in whatever magic they produced. There were gold-nibbed fountain pens with pots of ink writing the perfect love letter, charcoal and pencils sketching fantastic scenes that were ejected as soon as they were finished, one by one, into a machine that chewed them up, smoothed them into a new sheet of paper, and presented them back to the pencils for a new sketch.

Tourmaline looked longingly at them, turning her head as they passed. The homework she did for Professor Sharma would surely turn out better if she had one of those pens.

"What do you think that is?" Mai pointed at a seemingly empty glass case labelled 'Air of Discontent', but neither Tourmaline nor George answered. They had run past her and were staring at a multicoloured octopus who was staring back at them from a huge glass case that had been turned into a tank.

"What do you think she does?" whispered Tourmaline. She was wondering if the water was actually Source, and remembering how it had felt when she was swimming around in it.

"I'm not sure I want to know," said George. The octopus was eyeing him in a way that made him wonder if she was thinking about lunch, although he knew for a fact that octopuses did not eat boys.

Tourmaline frowned. "Don't get distracted, George. Ooh, look! It's the watch!" She waved at Mai and they both looked at the pocket watch that had first been used by Evelyn Coltsbody to freeze Tourmaline at the centre of the maze on the island and afterwards by Mai to freeze Evelyn Coltsbody.

"How did that get here?" asked George. "Didn't the AICMA confiscate it to stop anyone using it?"

Tourmaline shook herself a bit at the memory of it being used on her.

"Wait," said Mai. "You don't think this place is owned by rogue hunters who stole it back, do you?" She sounded as though she thought that would be quite exciting.

But Tourmaline had already moved on.

George followed his friend, paused again, then dragged his gaze away from a dolls' house through the windows of which he swore he could see tiny figures moving.

They passed a glass case which contained a velvet-lined box with a selection of sailing instruments in it. Thanks to her trip on *The Hunter*, Tourmaline was able to recognize them.

"Oh!" said Mai. "There's an astrolabe and a quadrant

and just *look* at that spyglass. Dexta would *love* that."

Tourmaline looked at her friend and acknowledged that maybe she hadn't paid quite as much attention to the art of sailing as Mai had while they'd all been aboard Captain Violet's ship.

"Can you imagine how these things must have come into contact with the Source?" Mai's face was pressed right up to the glass with her hands either side. "Explorers must have made their way to the island just like we did! Or maybe there was a shipwreck, or maybe— Is that a nocturnal? I think it is!"

"Yes, yes," said Tourmaline, who had no idea. Suddenly she stopped, her expression alert. "But what about this?"

At the end of the aisle there was a single glass case, separate from the others in the row. There was only one magical artefact in the case. It sat on a small lectern, and for some reason she couldn't explain, it was calling to her.

On the lectern sat a single, large, beautifully bound book. It was sky blue with gilt edges in a seashell pattern.

The others had gathered around Tourmaline.

"That looks special," said Mai.

"But there's no title on the front," said George.

Tourmaline's heart beat faster at the thought of what she'd already decided she was going to do – which was to open one of the display cases in the Museum of Marvels. "I really think," she said, as she started looking for a way to get inside the glass case, "that I need to look at this properly."

"Good idea," said Celandine. "While there's nobody else here."

Mai stood on tiptoe to look on top of the case, which was too high for Tourmaline to see over.

"Tourmaline," said George, "I don't think this is a very good—"

"You're probably right, George, but we came here for a reason, and that reason is finding a way to stop my magic. The postcard said this place could help me, and the help we need is going to be in a book." She was still searching for a way to open the case. "And this is a book. But we can't very well read it when it's in a glass case, can we?" Tourmaline held her hands out as though she had absolutely no choice in the matter.

George looked both ways down the empty aisles,

thought about explaining further why opening a locked display case in a museum was a disastrous idea, then used his breath for a lengthy sigh instead. Nothing was going to change what was about to happen.

Tourmaline, having interpreted the sigh, gave George's arm a quick squeeze. "We're only going to have a quick look," she said consolingly. "No one will ever know."

George's eyes, ears and nerves were already on high alert, as they always were when Tourmaline did something like this. "It does seem promising," he conceded.

"Got it!" Tourmaline had started searching underneath the glass case and suddenly the front of it popped open. She jumped back up, and before George could protest, she slid the panel aside.

Celandine leaned in eagerly to touch the book. Tourmaline pushed her hand away. "George should do it," she said. "He's good with books. George, why don't you take a look at it?"

George didn't think a person could be good with books. They weren't animals or small children. Still, it did look enticing. And if any magical artefact was worth looking at, it was surely a book.

He opened it carefully.

Then frowned in puzzlement. "It's empty."

"What do you mean, empty?" Tourmaline peered over his shoulder.

"Blank," said George.

He riffled through the pages but the entire book was clean page after clean page.

"Maybe it's written in invisible ink and we're supposed to hold a flame under the pages," said Mai. "Or maybe only the people who work here can read what it says. Or *maybe* because it's a magical artefact, we just have to figure—"

"Tourmaline," said George suddenly. "You do it." He ushered Tourmaline into the space where he had been standing.

Tourmaline didn't say anything else but she had noticed that ever since she'd opened the case, her hands had been tingling. The closer she got to the book, the more they prickled all over. As she reached for it, they flared with light, illuminating the case, the book and her own face.

Celandine made an impressed sound. Tourmaline opened the book. On the title page, large, rather splotchy letters appeared as she read:

The Compendium of Everything.

George gave a squeak of wonderment that said he had completely changed his mind about how good an idea it had been to open the glass case. "You know what this means, don't you?" He was so excited he grabbed Tourmaline's arm and shook it, jostling her back and forth.

"I do mostly know what *The Compendium of Everything* means," said Tourmaline. "But you can tell me again if you want to."

George stopped shaking her arm and did a little hop instead. "It's a compendium! I've got one about the Battle of the Queens, and it tells you *everything*."

"So this one is everything about ... everything?" Tourmaline tilted her head to look at the size of the book. It was dauntingly large, but it didn't seem big enough for that.

"It's magical!" George was practically shouting. "And so are you! I think the compendium will tell us about whichever subject we want it to."

Tourmaline looked at the compendium, and at the writing that hadn't been there before she touched it.

"So it can tell me how to control my magic? How to stop it if I want to?"

"Maybe there's something about people who fell into the Source in there," said Mai.

Tourmaline looked back at the compendium and then turned the first page.

Contents
Part 1: Myths and Legends
Part 2: The Source of All Magic
Part 3: Magical Artefacts and
*   their Applications*

George was absolutely beside himself. He and Tourmaline exchanged a delighted glance. "Part Two," he said "Part Two. But then all the rest."

Tourmaline eagerly flipped to the right page. Again it was blank. She waited a second, then touched the page. Nothing happened. George took her hands and put them both palm down on the pages as though they were making handprints.

"Ask it," Mai whispered. She was looking over Tourmaline's shoulder.

Tourmaline cleared her throat. "Could you tell us about the Source of all magic please?"

Writing started to appear, line after line of tiny, spidery letters racing across the page and on to the next.

Tourmaline tried to keep up but George leaned in to read, so after a minute she gave up and moved out of the way. The book had sped on to the next page and George was making lots of oohing and aahing noises.

Tourmaline turned to Mai. "How did you know we had to ask?"

"Well," said Mai, "you get one question with trees and trees make paper and paper makes books, so I thought it might be the same sort of thing."

Tourmaline nodded. "What does it say, George?"

George was reading faster than he'd ever read before.

And then suddenly the writing stopped and, *poof*, it was gone, a small amount of black dust that disappeared into the air.

George blinked several times and coughed. "We're right about the Source making magical artefacts and about the magic not lasting forever," he said. "But nobody's ever fallen into the Source before. At least, the book didn't say anything about it."

There was a moment of silence, then George coughed again and rubbed his nose. "I don't think there's ever been anyone like you before, Tourmaline."

"Oh," said Tourmaline.

"Sorry," said George.

"Maybe it says more in the other parts," said Mai.

"Let's do Myths and Legends," said George.

Tourmaline took a breath and flipped the pages again. "Show me the legend," she said. Then added, "*Slowly*, please."

The legend of the lost city.
Long ago, a land of magic existed in the world, but it was torn asunder and lost to time.

"Torn asunder?" Tourmaline looked in puzzlement at George.

George shrugged. "It means it's not part of our world any more."

Mai made an impatient noise. "This isn't going to help. It's just talking about Elsewhere. Try the bit about magical artefacts."

At that second the words poofed off the page again. Mai wafted her hand in front of her face and George sneezed.

"Oh," said Tourmaline, whose curiosity had been piqued. "Was there more? Please?" She waited, but no more words appeared.

George suddenly grasped her arm. "Be careful. What if it is like trees and you only get one question?"

"What does that mean?" asked Celandine.

"We learned it when we were on the island of Elsewhere," said Mai. "You only get to ask a tree one question – that's what the tree said, anyway."

Celandine's eyes were bright and round as chocolate coins.

"I think," said Mai, "that George might be mostly

right, only the book is made from more than one tree."

George's eyebrows shot up. "Yes! So we get more than one question, but—"

"We won't know how many," said Tourmaline. "Because we don't know how many trees made the book."

She thought carefully. "We should ask about magical artefacts, then. If I sort of *am* one."

Tourmaline turned the pages carefully, pressing her lips together so she didn't accidentally ask any more questions. But before she could ask anything – accidental or otherwise – something made her stop. "Oh!"

Mai let out a sound of disbelief. "Is that a—?"

"Postcard!" said Tourmaline. She reached for it, then pulled her hand back. She wanted to see the picture properly this time. She pulled her sleeve over her hand and used that to take it out from between the pages where it had been nestled.

"It *can't* be for you," said George.

But when Tourmaline turned it over, there was her name, in the same handwriting as the other two cards.

Everyone made suitable sounds of wonder and George looked round warily, as though the mystery postcard author might be right behind them.

"Read it, then," said Celandine, trying to see over Mai's shoulder.

I've helped you for free,
Now will you help me?
The thing I most need,
Is to be truly freed.

Your turn, Tourmaline.

Tourmaline quickly glanced at the picture on the front, but it was a plain white card.

She was just about to touch it to see what magical picture would appear when a sound came from somewhere in the museum. George's hands shot out, one to grab Tourmaline's arm and the other Mai's. His face was a picture of alarm, even more so when Tourmaline nearly knocked the book off its stand.

She clapped her other hand on top of it, then carefully disengaged George, righting the book before quietly closing the glass case. She hastily shoved the postcard into her satchel.

At the end of the aisle a woman passed by. Tourmaline froze. But before anyone had time to do anything, the woman backtracked, looking down the aisle straight at the children.

"What in all of Escea," she said, in a clipped manner, "are four children doing at AICMA headquarters?"

Chapter Seventeen

"AICMA headquarters?" George's voice was so faint the woman at the other end of the aisle couldn't possibly have heard it. But Tourmaline heard – and felt – every speck of the horror in his words.

She looked at him and found that she was shaking her head. They couldn't possibly be in AICMA headquarters. They were in the Museum of *Marvels*. It was full of *magical* artefacts. It was hidden by *magic*.

There were several tense moments where they all stared at each other, the woman blinking behind her spectacles.

And then it all started to make a horrible sort of sense to Tourmaline. The magical artefacts were the ones the Agency had found, taken, confiscated and collected over the years. They were locked away in glass cases to stop anyone from using them. Anyone except the Agency, that was, who didn't seem to have any problem with using a magical artefact to hide their own headquarters.

It was hypocritical of them to use magic when they went around telling everyone else that they *couldn't* use magic. That thought brought Tourmaline out of her shock, and she realized that they had come to the last place in all the world that she wanted to be. The most dangerous place for a magical girl who couldn't control if – and when – her magic was going to show itself.

This whirlwind of thoughts and feelings took a few seconds and made Tourmaline feel a bit dizzy. George looked mortified. But Celandine looked unbothered and Tourmaline wasn't about to have the new girl deal with this better than she was. She shook her head, stuffed her hands in her pockets and opened her mouth to start telling the best lies she could think of.

Before she could do that, (and it was just as well, because she really couldn't think of anything very good) Mai spoke first.

"Hello," said Mai breezily. "My mother works here. I'm Emiko Cravenswood's daughter and these are my friends. We're just waiting for my mother to finish something important and she said we could look around. I hope that's OK."

She strode forwards, widening her eyes at Tourmaline on the way past. Tourmaline scrunched her hands into fists inside her pockets and made a point of not looking back at the compendium.

George marvelled, not for the first time, at Mai's ability to lie so quickly and thoroughly.

"Emiko is here?" said the woman, though she still looked a little startled. "It's usually just me on weekends. I'm the curator of the museum."

"And now you have guests," said Mai, making it sound like that was a delightful occurrence.

"Guests?" said the neat little woman. "But I wasn't expecting guests..."

"We can go and wait for Emiko somewhere else," said Tourmaline. "We don't want to be any trouble."

George nodded hard at this. His palms were very sweaty and he wiped them on his jumper.

The curator clapped her hands together, making George jump. "Not at all," she said. "Where are my manners? Guests! It's been a very long time indeed since I had guests." She looked at each of the children in turn. She was a tidy person with careful hair and a cardigan, which she now brushed off with her small hands. "I'd be happy to answer any questions you have."

"Thank you. That would be lovely," said Tourmaline, not to be outdone in the lying department.

"I see you were admiring our latest acquisition," said the curator, leading them back down towards the compendium.

George shook his head, very minutely but very frantically. Tourmaline understood his panic but didn't see any way out of this except through.

"The ... book?" she said. "Yes, we all just love books so much. Is it new?"

"New to us," said the curator as they reached the case that had, very recently, been open. "But of course it's extremely old. Ancient in fact."

Tourmaline put her boot over some ink dust that was still on the floor. George covered his mouth, almost beside himself with worry.

"That's so interesting," said Tourmaline. "What does it do?"

She swiped her boot back firmly, kicking the dust behind them.

"Oh, it will take months of research to dig out all its secrets," said the curator. "But we have plenty of time and resources to devote to that. We think it might hold some very interesting information we can use in our work."

"Your work?" asked Celandine. Her face was the picture of rapt curiosity and interest.

The curator smiled down at Celandine's innocent elfin face. "We investigate and classify magical artefacts here," she said. "And once we've figured out what they can do, we destroy them. It's the mission of the Agency to rid the world of these dreadful things."

Tourmaline's toes suddenly felt quite cold. George was looking so worried that Mai gave him a soft thump on the arm to make him stop before the curator got suspicious.

"You destroy everything magical?" asked Celandine.

"Then why are there so many artefacts here?"

"These are the ones we haven't quite cracked yet," said the woman, rearranging her little cardigan. She indicated that they should carry on walking, taking a leisurely route down the next aisle. "But don't you worry – the minute we find out what they can do, they'll be decommissioned. We're here to keep you safe."

"Oh, good," said Celandine. She managed to sound really grateful and not as though she'd just come from a market that dealt solely in putting magic into the world. If Tourmaline hadn't been extremely busy trying to think of how to get away from this woman, she might have felt some grudging respect.

"If only we had some foolproof way of unlocking the magical secrets every time," the curator was saying. "Unfortunately they're quite stubborn and often fickle."

"You can't always figure out what they do?" asked Mai, casting a glance at Tourmaline.

"Not yet," said the curator. "But it's only a matter of time before we get our hands on some way of making them all work. Just think how much faster we could eradicate magic from the world then!"

George took hold of Tourmaline's hand and squeezed it very tight. And even though his hand was very damp and sweaty, Tourmaline squeezed right back.

"Now," said the woman, "why don't you follow me? I have something rather especially marvellous that I've been dying to show somebody, but of course the agents are always too busy." Here she looked at Mai. "I'm sure your mother must be working extremely hard where she's stationed. Is that why she's here on the weekend?"

"Oh, yes. You know how it is," said Mai, as if she was party to all the ins and outs of her mother's job and had not, in fact, only found out what Emiko did a few short weeks ago.

The curator led them along the end of the aisles across to the far side of the museum. Several doors led off to offices and other rooms that contained various tanks, tubes and an array of instruments. It looked like intriguing experiments might be conducted inside them.

George craned his neck to see into one of the rooms and the curator smiled. "For investigating," she said. "And classifying."

The curator stopped in front of a closed door, then opened it with a flourish and a look of proud anticipation on her face.

She stood aside and ushered them through the door. The room was a large and very secure-looking lab. Tourmaline frowned and turned back to the curator, who was still outside the room. "What is it that's so marvellous?"

The curator frowned at her over the top of her glasses. "That any of you thought that I would, for one second, buy that ridiculous story of yours."

She closed the door swiftly and the children heard several heavy mechanisms clanking into place.

Chapter Eighteen

Tourmaline ran to the door and rattled the knob fiercely. She had been in this position before, though, and had some experience of finding that locked doors really were locked.

Slowly, she turned round to face the others.

"I don't think she believed you," she said to Mai.

"No," said Mai. "But I did my best."

"It's not your fault," said Tourmaline. "You were excellent, really."

George heaved a sigh – both at the locked-in situation and the fact that his two best friends spent so much of their time lying in the first place.

Tourmaline did a quick circuit of the lab, pulling at a bookcase and tugging at random books in case there were any hidden doors or secret passages. Disappointingly, there were none.

Mai tried the door again then called out loudly, "Hello?"

"Don't!" said George. "Do we really want her to come back?"

"Of course not," said Celandine. "What we want is to be long gone before she returns."

"And just how are we supposed to do that?" Tourmaline demanded.

"Same way as you got out of Winona's tent?"

There was a pause.

"Oh," said Tourmaline.

George's face brightened considerably, which made it extra disappointing when the coin wouldn't work at all. Tourmaline got quite red in the face with all the concentrating, but nothing she did made any difference. The lock wouldn't budge.

"What are we going to *do*?" she said, pulling at her curls with both hands.

"We can't let them find out that you're *magic*," said George, whispering the last word as he glanced around warily.

"I know!" said Tourmaline. "We all heard what she said about finding something that can make the magical artefacts work, and *I'm that thing*."

"At least they don't know we used the compendium," said Mai.

Tourmaline paused, still tugging at her hair. "I think I left it open instead of closing it."

George's eyes widened. "You didn't."

"I did a bit," said Tourmaline, swallowing.

"She definitely did," said Celandine.

"The curator's going tell my mother," said Mai.

George's worry expanded into full panic. "Your mother's going to tell *my mother*."

"We just have to get out of here before the curator comes back," said Tourmaline. She looked around the lab. It was a large room, and although there were no windows and only one, locked, door, there had to be something that could help.

"Let's search," she said, and made a beeline for a small fridge in the corner by a sink and a kettle.

"Good idea," said Mai. "There has to be something here that can help us."

"What if there isn't?" asked George. "What if we're just stuck?"

No one acknowledged George's worries that this was a dire situation, because at that moment, Tourmaline gave a cry of triumph and turned round holding several sandwiches wrapped in foil.

George clasped his hands together and closed his eyes for a moment. He had been so hungry that everything was starting to look even bleaker than it actually was – and that was quite bleak enough.

"I *knew* this was the right thing to do," said Tourmaline, taking a huge bite of thick, seeded bread. "We'll be out of here in no time."

There followed several minutes of chewing and sighing and licking of fingers and finding of crumbs.

"Let's see that last postcard again," said George.

Tourmaline took her satchel off, pulled out the postcard with her sleeve over her hand again, and laid it on a bench. They all stared at it – maybe the most impossible postcard of all.

"How can the postcard sender possibly have known that I'd open the compendium?" Tourmaline asked.

She shook her head, thoroughly baffled.

"When do you think they put it there?" said George. "Before we came or ... were they watching us?" He looked around the room again as though he expected someone to walk through one of the walls.

"Could they be using magic?" said Mai breathlessly. "Maybe a crystal ball. Or a magic mirror to spy on us."

George was still looking round the room warily. "Whoever's doing this must be very clever. I don't like it. I don't like it at all."

Tourmaline loved a good plan, but most of hers were thought up on the spur of the moment. Whoever had done this was a most excellent planner – perhaps someone who could read her mind to know exactly what she was going to do before she even did it.

She was just wondering if it was really possible – magically speaking – to read someone's mind, when Celandine said impatiently, "Are you going to find out what the picture is?"

Tourmaline instantly wished that she didn't have to do exactly that. Or that she'd thought to do it before Celandine had suggested it. But of course, she *had* to know what the picture clue was this time.

She pressed her hand to the face of the card. Her fingertips glowed, and a picture of a doorway appeared. It was filled with a solid and very serious door.

"Is that it?" said George. "What are we supposed to do? That door could be anywhere."

Mai flipped the card over and read it again.

I've helped you for free,
Now will you help me?
The thing I most need,
Is to be truly freed.

Your turn, Tourmaline.

"The postcard sender is locked up?" Mai looked cautious, which was rare. "Do you think they're locked up behind the door?" Her eyes widened. "And if they are, then *why*? Maybe they're *dangerous*. Maybe they're not even a person. Maybe it's a magical monster."

Tourmaline thought for a moment. "Then how are

they sending the postcards?"

Mai's eyes were still wide. "*Magic*."

"You mean they're like me?" said Tourmaline, keeping her voice hushed. "It's someone magical so they've been locked up?"

Mai shrugged. "Maybe."

"But they must be right here in this building," said Tourmaline. "Why else would the door be the next clue? And if they're locked up here, then they really might be like me."

"I think you're right, Tourmaline," said George.

Tourmaline smiled and thought that if she had to be locked up somewhere by dreadful adults for the second time in as many days, then she was very lucky to be locked up with such good friends. She tucked the postcard into her pocket and looked at the remains of the food (which was largely crumbs at this point).

"I wish there had been cake," said Mai.

"I know," said Tourmaline, finishing off a large bottle of apple juice she'd also found. "What kind of people don't have cake?" She shook her head. The kind of people who thought magic should be destroyed, she supposed.

She looked around anew, feeling much better. There were thick, protective suits with visors, and gloves and boots hanging on the walls. Lab equipment like flasks, vials, tubes and chemicals was either out on the counters or in cupboards underneath. Spread on the benches around the perimeter of the room were an assortment of vices and tools. Notebooks lay open next to various items. Someone had clearly been conducting tests on them and recording the findings.

Following the snacks, everyone was much more motivated to make a thorough search of the room. Mai climbed up on the counters and peered on to high shelves. Celandine rummaged through the cupboards. George leafed through the notebooks while Tourmaline walked around the room, poking at the equipment and tools, hefting chisels and pliers in her hands and eyeing the door.

"They're not having much luck making these magical artefacts work," he said. He had already noted, with some satisfaction, that the Agency's experiments were no more successful than his own had been when he had been trying to find out about Tourmaline's magic.

They had dissected magical artefacts and made notes on what happened. Sometimes the artefacts had worked and sometimes they hadn't. The agents had made notes on that too, though they couldn't seem to find a reason this was happening.

"Here," he said, holding out a child's toy train. "See if you can make it work, Tourmaline."

"That's not going to get us out of here," said Tourmaline.

"It's worth a try, there's nothing useful up here," said Mai, jumping down from the counter.

Tourmaline sighed and took the train from George. "Did you try the switch on the side?" She flicked the switch, and as she did, her hands gave off a pulse of light. The train's wheels whirred and then spun frantically, spinning off her fingers as she dropped the thing with a cry.

The train roared round the room, shot up the cupboards at an impossible, vertical angle and rampaged across a countertop, churning up notebook pages in its wake. It raced off the counter into the sink where it continued to zoom, turning on its side in a circle and whipping the left-behind washing-up water into a foam.

Celandine let out a small giggle. And although they were all captive again and there was no Persephone or anyone else coming to help this time, Tourmaline couldn't help but laugh too.

George managed a smile. "Maybe," he said, "even though this place is just as terrible as the Dark Market, it can still help us too."

"We know from the compendium that no one else ever fell into the Source," said Tourmaline. "So if there's never been anybody like me before, we'll have to find out how to fix me some other way."

George nodded. "We know you amplify magical artefacts. We know you can make them work if they weren't working before. We know that these things happen when your hands glow, but we *also* know that magical things happen around you even when your hands *don't* glow."

Tourmaline looked at her hands. "Do you think the glowing part is important?"

George raised his eyebrows questioningly at his friend. "Do you?"

Tourmaline thought about all the times her magic had caused trouble. About every time it had done anything at all. "I think it is," she said. "You're right. But I can't quite..." There was something there in her mind – something she couldn't reach. Like a bumblebee bumbling around a flower, the idea wouldn't quite land. It was something to do with the glowing, or the times that she didn't glow, but she couldn't quite work it out.

Celandine had been searching among the other items on the bench and suddenly she turned round holding something. "What about this key? The notebook says they can't figure out what it opens."

Four pairs of eyes shot to the door.

Tourmaline took the key eagerly. Her fingers gave a little shiver of light.

She ran to the door with the glowing key, ready to save the day. "Where's the...?"

She heaved a sigh. "There's no lock to put it in." The door was secured by some other mechanism that must have been hidden inside it. The outer surface was smooth.

Celandine had a look anyway. Tourmaline frowned

while she did – as though she herself didn't know a keyhole when she saw one.

George, meanwhile, had noticed a folder hanging from a loop by the door and was flicking through it.

"I think I know why the lucky coin didn't work to get us out of here," he said. "And why you wouldn't be able to use that key even if there was a keyhole." He held up what he had been reading – a thick manual with the title *Protocols for Protection from Magic*. "It says this lab has been constructed so that no magic can escape from it, in case they have a very powerful magical artefact, or one they can't control. It's supposed to protect all the other agents in the building who aren't working in the lab."

At that moment, there was a scuffling commotion outside the door. The sounds were muffled, but it was, unmistakeably, several people. Tourmaline stuffed the key in her pocket, backing away from the door hastily. George looked round desperately for anything that they had missed that could help. Someone was coming and the children were out of time.

Chapter Nineteen

"Is it the curator?" whispered George, his eyes round.

"If it is, she's brought someone with her. Several someones," said Tourmaline grimly. "But I'm not letting them take us away, or whatever it is that they want to do, before I get what I came here for." She looked around the room again. "What about this?" There was a vent under one of the counters.

Mai looked at it doubtfully. "Where does it go? Is it big enough?"

"Yes," said George, his eyes on the door. "It's perfect."

Celandine grabbed a screwdriver and got to work on the vent. Not to be outdone, Tourmaline snatched up a small crowbar and prised the vent opening off just as the door mechanisms started unlocking.

"Hurry up!" said George. He shot forwards and Tourmaline bundled him into the vent first, pushing in after so that Mai and Celandine could follow. They all scrambled forwards on hands and knees just as the door to the lab opened behind them.

Tourmaline took a brief moment to feel very satisfied that not only had they escaped, but she had made the magical artefacts in the lab work when the agents couldn't. Not to mention the fact that they'd eaten everyone's lunch.

It was dark in the vent but they crawled on quickly. The thought of getting caught again made George a lot faster than anyone had known he could be.

"I'm sorry I couldn't help us with magic," whispered Tourmaline. "You would have thought in a place full of magical artefacts I could have managed something."

"A non-magical escape is just as good as a magical one," said George. "You can't solve *everything* with magic."

Mai nodded and banged her head on the upper surface of the vent. "Sometimes you just have to use vents, even if it does bruise your head and your knees. The important thing is the escaping."

"We are going to be able to get *out* of the vents, though, aren't we?" asked Celandine from the back.

"Of course we are," said Tourmaline. "But I'm not going home until I've found out exactly what my magic does and how to be in charge of it. I'm finding that door and whoever's been sending me the postcards."

She sounded so certain that George picked up the pace even more. After several minutes of crawling, though, he stopped.

"What is it?" asked Tourmaline.

"I've found another vent," George whispered. "I'm listening to see if anyone's outside it in the room."

Tourmaline grew impatient in the silence that followed, then there was a sharp, tinny pop and light shone in. George had pushed the vent off.

"I did it," he said, sounding both pleased and surprised.

"George, you can do lots of things," said Tourmaline. "Now hurry up and move, my knees hurt."

They crawled out into a large boardroom with a long wooden table in the middle of it with six chairs on either side. Several other doors led off from the room but they were closed. There were boards lining the walls.

And every board was covered, from floor to ceiling, with maps, written notes, pictures, note cards with questions written on them and diagrams linked together with arrows, pins and red string.

No one said anything for a few moments as the four children took it all in.

"Is that Captain Violet?" asked Mai, peering up at a picture on the wall. The captain was mid-roar, her gold tooth flashing, being restrained by two scared-looking men. The picture was linked by red string to three other, smaller ones of the rest of the crew. Quintalle's was quite blurred, but you could still see her ferocious scowl as she advanced on whoever was taking the picture.

Suddenly Tourmaline darted forwards. "It's Pellavere!" There were diagrams and blueprints and notes along with a lengthy description of the Archive and the many difficulties of interviewing the Living Archives.

"And this is about the Dark Market," said Celandine from the other side of the room.

"I think this bit is about the island of Elsewhere," said George.

"It's all the magical places in the world!" said Tourmaline.

Celandine scoffed. "All the ones *they* know about, anyway."

"They need to put themselves up on this wall," said Tourmaline, "if they're going to use magic to hide their headquarters."

"They didn't do a very good job of that, anyway," said Celandine. "We found it, didn't we?"

The two girls looked at each other and almost smiled.

"I can't believe all these places are magical," said George, staring round the room in wonder.

"I can't believe my mother works here," said Mai.

They darted about, exclaiming at pictures or notes that had been pinned up.

It was all so very detailed and so very interesting – like a whole new world opening up right in front of them.

Tourmaline walked slowly round the room, her hands behind her back and her face alight with possibility. Seeing all these magical places had given her a very strong sense of what she wanted to do when she grew up and, truth be told, she wasn't sure it could wait that long.

Every one of the places on the walls sounded wondrous. For the Agency, they might have been possible targets to seek out, investigate, classify and then destroy, but to her they were adventure and discovery, travel and magic.

There was a long list of names pinned up too – Evelyn Coltsbody's name was at the top and someone had stuck a star next to it. Tourmaline stared at it and had some complicated feelings that she decided to put away and examine later.

Mai came to see what Tourmaline was looking at. "Captain Violet and the crew are on this list too!" she said, pointing them out. "They're quite high up," she added, sounding almost proud. "Wait a minute, has something been torn off here?"

She touched the bottom of the list, which had been ripped in an uneven line. All that remained, was the letter 'y'. It looked as though it had been at the end of whatever had been removed.

"Do you think there was another name here?" asked Mai.

Tourmaline barely heard her. "Look how many people

there are," she said. "There must be magical places all over the world! And all these people *live* in that world."

It made her feel as though her magic might be part of something bigger. And as though that might be a wonderful thing (even if the list was pinned up so these people could be taken into custody just like Evelyn Coltsbody had been).

"Tourmaline," said Mai, a bit more sharply. "It's a name ending in 'y'. Just like Tourmaline *Grey*."

"What?" Tourmaline's eyes widened in alarm. "Do you think they already know about me?"

"We should hurry up," said Celandine, suddenly behind them. "Let's get out of here."

"But what if—" Tourmaline's worries were interrupted by a small sound from outside the room, somewhere deep in the building.

Tourmaline spun round – everyone else had heard it too. They had alert, listening faces.

"Let's go somewhere less important-looking," said Tourmaline, leading them swiftly to one of the other doors in the room. She pulled it open and peeked in. The sounds outside were getting closer.

"The curator's coming with lots of agents!" said George.

The room Tourmaline had found was a sort of reference library – a long thin room with floor-to-ceiling bookshelves on both sides, but it was empty and there was a door at the other end of it, so they could get away. Tourmaline led them inside and Mai closed the door quietly behind them – just as someone entered the boardroom. Mai froze, her hand still on the door knob.

Tourmaline put her finger to her lips and opened the door at the other end. Or at least, she tried. It wouldn't open. She turned round to see George's anxious face. Mai pushed past Celandine and tried it herself.

"It's locked," she said quietly. She gave it a good hard yank. "It really is. We *can't* be trapped again."

"We're not," said Tourmaline in a very determined way.

She searched in her pockets, a look of triumph on her face as she pulled out what she'd been looking for – the magical artefact she'd taken from the AICMA lab.

The key shone in the glowing light from her fingers the instant Tourmaline pulled it out of her pocket.

And worked like a charm the second she put it into the door.

"I told you," said George. "You really can make any magical artefact work." He sounded both relieved and confident as the lock clicked.

Tourmaline removed the key and waved it in the air. "I'm getting good at this, aren't I?" The key had its key-ness and Tourmaline had her Tourmaline-ness, and between one wanting to open locks and the other determined to make that happen, the magic had worked.

As she waved the key, though, in the narrow room, the back of her fingers brushed the books on the shelf and something she hadn't intended at all happened.

There was a shuffling sound, like sheets of paper being moved. After that, everything happened very quickly.

The books flapped their way off the shelves by the handful, whirling to the floor like sycamore seeds, their pages whirring open one by one, back and forth, faster and faster as though people were flicking through every book at top speed at the same time.

Celandine dodged nimbly out of the way. George ducked into a corner, his hands over his head. Mai made a grab for the door, getting tangled up with Tourmaline.

The chaos made the most tremendous amount of noise and went on for quite some time during which there was nothing to be done about it.

As it died down, the children looked at each other, wide-eyed and horror-struck. The bookshelves were empty. The books were strewn over the floor like a kaleidoscope of butterflies. One of them gave a last flutter of its pages.

Tourmaline shrugged helplessly to let everyone know that she hadn't meant that to happen. Her fingers had stopped glowing so she had no idea why the magic had done what it had just done.

From the other side of the door in the boardroom, there was silence, followed by a low voice saying something and another answering it.

Tourmaline's head tilted to the side, listening. Carefully, slowly, she stepped through the books, back towards the door they had come through.

218

"Tourmaline, what are you doing?" asked George, from his corner.

Tourmaline reached for the door, looking, alarmingly, as though she was going to open it.

"Don't!" said Mai.

Tourmaline shook her head. "I recognize those voices from somewhere. I know it."

"But what if—?" George never got the chance to ask what would happen if it was the curator – or someone much worse – because the door was already open.

Tourmaline peered back into the boardroom and stopped stock still in shock. "What are *you* doing here?"

Chapter Twenty

"Captain Violet?" said Tourmaline.

"Oh! It was you lot outside the lab, not the curator," said Mai.

"*The* Captain Violet?" asked Celandine, her eyes growing even wider. "Captain of *The Hunter*?"

"The very same," said the captain, doffing her hat and flashing her gold tooth.

"But what are you doing here?" asked Tourmaline.

The captain looked perfectly innocent, but behind her Tourmaline saw the crew exchanging glances.

"What are *you* doing here?" asked the captain. "And what happened in there?" She pointed to the catastrophe in the library behind the children.

"Nothing," said Tourmaline. "I asked you first."

"We're working," said Captain Violet. "We've been hired to do a job."

"What job?" asked Tourmaline suspiciously. The captain and her crew were rogue hunters, on the list of the AICMA's most wanted, and the last place she would have expected to see them was the AICMA headquarters.

"Retrieving a valuable artefact for a client," said the captain.

Mai linked her arm with Tourmaline's. "What kind of artefact?"

George inched closer. "Which client?"

For a moment the four children stared at the crew with narrowed eyes and the four crew members tried not to look as though they'd just hit the jackpot.

"It's come to our attention that Tourmaline has become a ... high-value item, shall we say, in the hunting world."

"Tourmaline is not an item," said George, frowning.

The captain shrugged. "A commodity, then. The point is, she's worth a lot of money."

"To who?" demanded Celandine. The way she

crossed her arms looked a lot like Tourmaline did when she was in a demanding mood.

"To a contact of mine at the Dark Market," said the captain. She grinned at Tourmaline, her gold tooth shining. "I believe you've already met."

George suddenly took a breath. Tourmaline tugged on his sleeve to let him know that she wasn't about to let anyone lock them away again.

"So you came here to kidnap me?"

"That's the job we're *supposed* to do," said the captain, looking at Tourmaline thoughtfully.

"But – But you won't really do that," said George cautiously, "will you?"

"Of course I won't do that," said the captain.

George breathed a sigh of relief.

"As long as we get something better in return," said the captain.

Quintalle grunted, which was as close as she came to a positive sentiment. Miracle and Dexta were grinning.

Tourmaline sighed. "What do you want?"

"Quite a lot of things that we've seen here," said the captain.

"It really is a museum of marvels," added Dexta, flipping one of her sharp knives end over end and grinning.

"Oh," said Mai, "I saw a collection of nautical instruments that you would *love* and there's an *octopus*—"

"A live one?" asked Quintalle.

"Yes," said Mai. "I don't know what it does, though. Why?"

Quintalle shook her head so that all her gold earrings jangled. "I don't agree with animal cruelty," she growled.

Mai blinked. "Neither do I."

The captain suddenly clapped her hands together. "Well, lovely though this reunion is, we'd better be on our way, don't you think? The curator who went to raise the alarm about you breaking in here is currently locked in a small office. But I daresay she'll be able to make contact with other agents from there." She looked at Tourmaline with a certain amount of respect. "Good work on infiltrating this place, by the way. An excellent break-in."

"Thank you," said Tourmaline.

George nudged her arm, not very gently.

Tourmaline blinked. "I mean, we *didn't* break in. Not exactly. And if we had it wouldn't have been the right thing to do." She cast a sideways glance at her friend. "Even though the Agency is terrible and just as bad as the people at the Dark Market or probably worse, really."

"I find it's simpler not to worry about such things," said the captain.

"It makes our job easier," added Miracle.

"Anyway," said the captain, "the main thing is that we'd really like to leave before Agency reinforcements arrive."

Mai shrugged. "Fine. Go, then. Just leave us here, we've got things to do."

The captain and the crew exchanged looks.

"We've got things to do too," said Dexta.

"Like getting rid of all the information the Agency has in this room," said Miracle.

The captain nodded. "They know a lot more than we thought they did. Which, as you can imagine, is very inconvenient for us. Professionally speaking."

Tourmaline had a creeping suspicion that she wasn't going to like the answer to her next question, but she asked it anyway. "What are you going to do?"

"Me?" The captain laughed. It was more of a cackle really and it was so loud that George jumped.

"Not *me*," said Captain Violet. "No, it's been made very clear to me by Emiko Cravenswood that we, by which I mean myself and the crew, are not welcome, well, anywhere. And I suspect that if we were to be found in the vicinity of the AICMA headquarters, it might result in us finding that *The Hunter* had mysteriously been blown to smithereens, possibly with us on board."

"That would be a shame," said Tourmaline.

"The crew certainly think so," said Captain Violet. "And so, you see, we have no choice but to leave before the curator's reinforcements arrive. Which means, Tourmaline, it's *you* who needs to destroy all this evidence."

"And as mentioned, there are a few magical artefacts from that museum we've got our eye on," added Miracle.

"If I do this for you, you'll let me go?" asked Tourmaline.

She looked at George. He shook his head, a very slight movement that was nonetheless frantic. He mouthed, "You can't!"

Tourmaline tried to convey to George (with her eyes) that she had no choice. She *couldn't* go back to the Dark Market and work for Winona. But in truth, there was a fizz of excitement in her stomach. She *wanted* to stop the wonderful magical artefacts in the museum from being destroyed (especially the octopus, who deserved a lot more from life than that). She wanted to take down the list of the people in the magical world and go and meet them (carefully, in case they were awful like Winona). She wanted to learn about a world that she was now part of. She wanted to see it all.

"Judging by the devastation behind you, I don't think you'll find it too difficult." The captain spread her hands as though it were the easiest thing in the world.

Tourmaline crossed her arms. "And *then* you'll let us go?"

"I'll forget I ever saw you," said the captain. "You have my word."

Tourmaline wasn't sure how much that was really worth, but she didn't say so.

"I'll do it," she said.

"A pleasure doing business with you," said the captain.

"Don't forget the octopus," said Quintalle.

Dexta grinned and tossed a knife high up in the air before catching it again.

"There's only one way out of here and we'll be waiting right outside," said the captain. "Bring us everything on this list, because if you don't, we'll be forced to take Tourmaline instead."

Miracle had been scribbling on a piece of paper she'd pulled from the wall, and she handed it to George.

It was a list – a long one – of magical artefacts from the museum of marvels.

The captain doffed her hat, Dexta saluted and the whole crew left the room and disappeared silently into the building – and presumably very quickly out of it again to wait outside for the children.

"We don't have time for this," said Celandine. "We need to find that doorway from the postcard."

"I can't do that if I'm a prisoner," said Tourmaline. "Besides..." She tailed off, looking into the boardroom, a frown on her face.

"What?" asked George.

Tourmaline pointed across the room. "Who do you think is going to end up at the top of that list if we *don't* do this?"

There was a pause, before George suddenly walked off, right across the room, reached up and did something he'd never done before – he ripped the list (which didn't belong to him) off the wall (which was in an important room that belonged to important adults) and tore it into little bits. "Tourmaline's right," he said. "So we're doing it for her, not Captain Violet."

He moved his hand as though he was about to throw the little bits of paper into the air and let them rain down on the floor, but then stopped. He couldn't quite bring himself to go that far.

"For Tourmaline," Mai said as she joined him. "And the octopus." And she started tearing things down off the walls.

Celandine needed no encouragement at all, and happily went to work pulling off the red string that linked the big picture of Captain Violet to the pictures of Miracle, Dexta and Quintalle.

But Tourmaline stood back and looked. The room was so big and there was so much information. How were they even going to reach the things at the very top of the walls? They had to destroy all this information, collect the magical artefacts from the captain's list *and* find the postcard sender, whoever and wherever they were. It was all going to take far too long.

She opened one of the other doors that led off from the boardroom, and then another. She ended up in someone's office, where she found a fan. It was small and mechanical and when she saw it, she had an idea – a feeling in her fingers – of what a fan like that could do if you made it *more*. Maybe that feeling was telling her that the fan was a magical artefact. So she reached for it, and as she did it started whirring, at first spinning round slowly and then gaining speed. And as it did *that*, Tourmaline smiled.

"Everyone stand back," she said as she walked back into the boardroom.

Mai's face scrunched in confusion and then opened back up in delight. "Tourmaline, where did you find a—"

No one heard the rest of Mai's question as the roaring of the little fan turned into a storm. George's hair was blasted back as he struggled his way past it to stand behind Tourmaline. Mai and Celandine whooped and laughed as they joined him.

Tourmaline unleashed a surprising amount of devastation on the neat and orderly notes and the plans of the AICMA to squash magic and make the world a lot less interesting.

Small tornadoes whipped maps off the walls. Sudden upward whooshes of air blasted pictures and lists from beneath the pins that held them. The noise of tearing and falling and flapping filled the room until George covered his ears.

When it was over and the last note had settled like a falling leaf, Tourmaline put the fan down slowly and blinked. Her curls were a little windswept, and her expression startled, but she had a big smile on her face.

"No glowing," said George, nodding curiously to Tourmaline's hands. His voice sounded loud in the sudden silence.

"I know," said Tourmaline. "But we don't have time to talk about that now. Let's do the other thing the captain wants. And quickly. The curator might be locked up, but we don't know how long we have before the other agents come."

"George, do you have that list?" asked Tourmaline, as they strode through the empty corridors. Mai stopped at the lab and selected a large glass jar.

George pulled out the list and frowned at it. "I don't like this."

"It's not that bad," said Mai. "The AICMA are going to destroy the magical artefacts once they figure out what they do, anyway. If you think about it, we're saving them."

"Also," said Tourmaline, "the crew might not be able to make any of them work. It will be up to the magical artefacts whether they work or not."

That gave George a lot to think about in terms of there being a sliding scale of badness to everything. But what Tourmaline had said was also interesting. "Do you think the magical artefacts have a choice?"

Tourmaline shrugged. "I don't know, but everything on the island of Elsewhere had a reason for what it did, so I wondered if the magical artefacts did too. Maybe they don't work if someone wants them to do something bad."

George hurried forwards, suddenly feeling a lot better about the whole situation.

"What's first on the list?" said Tourmaline, when they reached the museum.

George opened his mouth.

"Let me out!" shouted a voice, muffled by the heavy door of one of the offices leading off from the display room. All the children jumped.

"At least we know where they locked the curator up now," said Mai. She had to raise her voice a bit over the hammering and thumping on the door.

"Oh dear," said George, looking anxious. "She sounds pretty angry."

"So will Captain Violet if we don't do this," said Tourmaline.

"Let's hurry up," said Celandine. "Whoever sent that postcard is waiting."

Tourmaline frowned at that. What did any of it matter to this girl? She would have liked to talk about it with George, but George was already scurrying up and down the aisles scanning the display cases and calling out items for the others to look for.

"Here!" shouted Mai. "Quintalle must have asked for this."

Tourmaline hurried to her friend and they carefully opened the case. The magical artefact inside was a perfectly ordinary-looking whisk. Tourmaline reached for it and Mai slapped her hand away.

"Sorry," she said as Tourmaline looked at her in surprise. "I just don't think we have time for you to set them all off. Let me." She picked up the whisk. "I bet this makes extra-delicious cakes. Or extra-*enormous* cakes. Tourmaline, I really want cake."

"Me too," said Tourmaline. But they didn't have to think about how delicious cake was (especially

Quintalle's chocolate cake) for very long, because, right at that second, George let out a terrified scream.

Chapter
Twenty-one

"George!" cried Tourmaline. She set off at a run.

Mai was close behind and by the time they reached him, Celandine was already there. Her short hair was sticking up and her expression was incredulous. George was shaking.

"I was standing right there," he said. He pointed, but nobody said anything for a moment, because nobody could believe what they were seeing.

"I was looking for a telescope and I found it *right there*," he said. He looked at Tourmaline helplessly.

Where a glass display case had been – apparently holding a telescope – there was now ... nothing. A cube of emptiness where *something*-ness had been before.

"I really don't like looking at it," said Mai, without

taking her eyes off it.

"It does make you feel a bit sick, doesn't it?" said Tourmaline.

"What did you do?" asked Celandine, managing to tear her eyes away and look at George.

"Nothing!" he said. "I didn't even open the case. I was just standing in front of it, I checked the list and I looked up again and it was—" He waved his hand, shook his head then made a noise. He couldn't explain this at all because no one possibly could.

"Maybe this is just what the telescope does?" said Mai doubtfully. She started backing away from the emptiness.

"You don't think it's going to happen again, do you?" asked George in alarm.

"Probably not," said Tourmaline reassuringly, but she took hold of his arm and pulled him back.

"Let's get away from it, whatever it is, and rescue the octopus," said Mai.

And they walked away, glancing back at the nothing warily.

At the octopus's tank, there were some moments of silence and frowning.

"How do we...?" Tourmaline tilted her head and looked at the creature in front of her, who was looking right back.

"I brought this," said Mai, lifting the glass jar. But the look on her face told the others that was as far as her plan had gone.

"There must be some way for them to feed her," said Celandine.

The octopus changed colour from a mottled blue-grey to a lime green.

"Oh," said Tourmaline. "Does the top open?"

The octopus became a pleasant shade of raspberry pink.

"This is strange," said Celandine. She started to climb up on top of one of the adjacent glass cases.

"Not really," said Tourmaline. "We've talked to trees before now, so why not an octopus?" She clambered up faster on the other side.

George and Mai exchanged a look.

Tourmaline paused. "You don't think," she said, "that the octopus could have been the one who – who sent the postcards?"

They all looked at the octopus, who turned faintly pink. George marvelled to himself that this wasn't even the strangest question someone had asked him that day.

"I suppose she could have—" Mai motioned writing. "With a tentacle."

Celandine scoffed. "The ink would have been smudged by the water," she said. "And how would she have delivered them to you? Gone for a walk to the post box?"

Tourmaline shook her head quickly. "You're right." Still, she eyed the creature suspiciously.

The octopus tapped one of her tentacles gently on the top of the tank.

"I think she's ready," said Mai. "Here." She held up the jar between the two other girls and both made a grab for it.

Celandine was faster – and Tourmaline's face did not need to change colour for Mai and George to know how she felt about it.

Tourmaline scowled as Celandine deftly opened the tank. She lowered the jar into the water so that it filled up, and the octopus – after examining the shape and size of the smooth glass with two of its tentacles – climbed straight in.

"I hope she's not too squished," said Mai, her eyebrows at a worried tilt as she took the jar from Celandine.

"It's only temporary," said George. He looked at it thoughtfully. "I think she's happy, anyway. She knows this is a rescue."

"I'll put her outside for the crew to collect," said Mai. She took the jar and ran off.

"What's next?" said Tourmaline.

Which was when the glass case that Celandine was perched on suddenly became nothing, gaping in a perfect rectangle where it had just been.

Celandine gave a cry as she fell. George let out a squeak. Tourmaline threw herself across the top of the tank of water between herself and Celandine and grabbed for the other girl's hands.

She caught them and the pair hung there for a second, Tourmaline's face almost in the water. Then Celandine scrabbled up the side of the tank. Tourmaline pulled and George tried to grab Celandine around the middle without getting too close to the emptiness.

Celandine put her foot on his shoulder and boosted herself on to the top of the water tank in such a panic that Tourmaline went in headfirst. Celandine went in after her and there followed a lot of splashing and shoving and spitting of water before the tank gave up and collapsed. The front pane of glass popped straight off and the water spilled out, the two girls tumbling on to the floor as George hopped back out of the way.

Both of them were breathing hard, dripping wet and looking shocked.

Tourmaline staggered to her feet, water pouring off her. She pushed her drenched curls out of her face and offered her hand to Celandine.

Celandine took it and stood up.

George gave a little gasp. He was staring down at Celandine's feet, where both of the girls now looked.

The tips of her shoes were gone.

Ten toes slowly uncurled. She wriggled them quickly and let out a big sigh of relief.

"Thank you, Tourmaline," she said, her voice breathless and quiet. "You caught me just in time."

"You're welcome," said Tourmaline, and she only sounded the tiniest bit smug. "But I think we have a big problem."

George nodded fervently. "We should leave. Immediately." Better to face Captain Violet and her many and various plans, or even Dexta and her knives, than the prospect of being blinked out of existence.

But Tourmaline held up a finger and raised her gaze. The faint thumps of the curator – now fewer and farther between – could still be heard.

George's eyes widened. "We have to let her out first! She probably won't even be *that* angry once she's sees what's happening."

At that moment, Mai came back. Her cheeks were flushed and her brown eyes had an expression that was more usually seen in George's – fear. "I dropped the whisk when George screamed so I went to get it on the way back and it's gone. There just a chunk of nothing."

George frowned. "What was in the case next to the octopus?"

"A dagger thing," said Mai, "with red jewels on the handle."

George consulted the list. "It's on here," he said.

"I bet Dexta wanted it," said Tourmaline, "and now it's gone."

"It's spreading," said Mai. She looked at the two other girls who were steadily dripping on to the floor. "What happened to you?"

Tourmaline pointed at the emptiness that Celandine had so recently almost become.

"At least the octopus is OK," said Mai. "She's with Quintalle."

"But the curator is still locked in," said Tourmaline. "Come on."

At the office door, Tourmaline paused. "Hello?" She knocked.

"What is happening out there?" asked a loud voice, very close to the other side of the door.

George clasped his hands together. The curator didn't sound any less angry than she had before.

"We've come to help," said Tourmaline, undaunted. "There's a bit of a … situation out here. A sort of disappearing-into-nothing situation." She took the magic key out of her pocket so that she could open the door.

There was a pause. "Oh dear," said the curator. "Oh no."

Tourmaline paused, the key almost at the lock. "What is it?" she asked. "Do you know what's happening?"

"Get me out of here at once," the curator demanded. "I have been bamboozled by ruffians and—"

"Yes, yes," said Tourmaline. "We *will* get you out. But—"

At that moment the door between them vanished entirely. The curator wobbled on the other side and then leaped back.

The peculiar quality of the nothing that was now between the woman and the children made them all blink. George put his hand on his stomach.

"Ah," said Tourmaline. "How is she supposed to get out now?"

Chapter
Twenty-two

The curator sighed and tucked her cardigan neatly around herself. "Well, this is unfortunate."

The emptiness that had been an oak door just moments before filled the space, (or *made* the space) between her and the children. It existed, queasily, even if it was ... nothing. It was hard to explain, and harder to look at. The walls of the office stretched up on either side – there was no way for the curator to leave the room.

"What do we *do*?" asked George in some distress. "I think the magic is disappearing everything now, not just the magical artefacts. We can't leave her here."

"We won't, George. I promise," said Tourmaline. "She's not the only person here, either, is she?"

George blinked.

"You know," said Tourmaline, widening her eyes. "The you-know-who, who sent the you-know-whats to me?"

"Oh!" said George. What with all the nothingness and octopuses and threats from the captain, he'd almost forgotten that they were there at the behest of the anonymous postcard sender. "Of course," he said. "Them too. Whoever they are, the postcard implied they were in this building and we can't just let this happen to them." He waved his hand at the emptiness. "We have to do *something*."

"What would Captain Violet do?" asked Celandine, checking behind them to see how much worse it was getting.

"I don't think that's a useful question to ask," said George quickly.

"At least not in this situation," added Tourmaline.

The curator pushed her glasses up her nose and sighed, as though she had decided something but didn't think it was a particularly good decision.

"I think I know why this is happening," she said.

"Although I'm not very keen on telling you."

"That doesn't matter," said Tourmaline cheerfully. "Nobody wants to tell us anything but we always find out anyway."

"It would be faster if you told us, though," added Mai.

"I believe this to be," said the curator, "the work of a particular magical artefact."

"Which one?" asked Tourmaline, glancing over her shoulder. Maybe they could take it and throw it out of the building into the clearing outside, like a magical grenade.

"That's where we run into a problem," said the curator. "I don't exactly know."

Tourmaline turned fully around and looked in dismay at the vast museum and every item that was still in it.

"What I mean," said the curator, "is that it's not in here."

"Then where is it?" asked Tourmaline impatiently.

"I don't know that either. I'm only the curator, you know. Some things are above my pay grade. Need-to-know only. Top-secret, you understand."

"No, I *don't* understand," said Tourmaline. "Are you telling me that we're looking for *something*, that is *somewhere*?"

The curator's frown cleared. "Yes," she said, with a neat nod of her head. "That's it exactly."

"That's helpful," muttered Celandine, just as Tourmaline said, "Wonderful," under her breath.

"If we're going to find it, we'd better hurry up," said Mai. She pointed and George made a sound that was half terrified and half disappointed. There was a large block of nothing where the compendium had once been.

"I was going to say we should ask the compendium," said George. "It was my only idea."

"Oh dear," said the curator sadly. "I was hoping that one day I might crack the code on that one, so to speak."

"You've never read it?" asked Tourmaline.

"No," said the curator, narrowing her eyes. "Why do you ask? And why are you dripping wet?"

"We have to go," said Tourmaline. "No time to waste. And don't worry," she called over her shoulder as she hastened away. "We'll definitely find the magical artefact and stop it and we won't leave you here!"

George hurried after Tourmaline before the curator

asked any more awkward questions, Mai and Celandine following. They barrelled down several corridors, looking for, well, they weren't sure what, but if it was that important surely they would notice.

As they ran past the devastation in the boardroom and library, Tourmaline glanced inside and saw that óne entire wall of the room was gone – consumed by nothing. The effect made her feel quite dizzy and sick and she tugged George forwards before he could see.

She wasn't sure if it was disastrous that so much of the room was gone, or possibly a bit of luck, since nobody would notice the havoc she'd caused with a little desk fan.

As she thought about this, looking this way and that into offices and cupboards, she knew that everything that had happened in the museum was telling her something about her magic. Something huge and important that she just didn't have time to think about in the proper way (aided by biscuits) at that moment.

Once they were deep inside the building, they came to a set of steps that went both up and down.

"Up," said Tourmaline decisively.

At the same time, Celandine said, just as decisively, "Down."

Tourmaline frowned. "Everyone knows the most important things are kept *up*."

Celandine frowned right back. "What about buried treasure?"

There was a stony silence during which Tourmaline tried furiously to come up with a retort.

"I think down too," said Mai.

George looked cautiously between his best friend and Celandine. Tourmaline's freckles looked particularly frustrated.

"Down," he said carefully. "Because otherwise it will be two against two and we don't have time for that."

Tourmaline huffed. "I *suppose* we can look there, if everyone wants to." But once Mai and Celandine had bolted down the stairs, she squeezed George's hand to let him know it was all right and he gave her a small smile.

At the bottom of the stairs, which wound down for some way, there was large door with a sign on it that said:

Clearance Level 7. DO NOT ENTER.

Underneath, in smaller letters, it said:

Items not to be removed from the bunker.
Do not take to lab under any circumstances.

This sign was handwritten. The writing was faded and a little bit shaky.

They exchanged glances. This looked promising. Terrifying, but promising. Not that Tourmaline was keen on admitting that Celandine might have been right.

But promising or not, it was a very solid door, and very locked. It didn't have a keyhole, just a control panel of some kind. Tourmaline was getting very fed up with locked doors and the people who kept locking them.

She threw her hands up. "I don't have Clearance Level One, never mind Seven."

"And you don't need it," said Celandine.

For the first time, Tourmaline noticed that the other girl was wearing a pair of trousers with a substantial number of pockets. She found herself admiring them so much it caused a greenish-feeling twinge in her toes. And when Celandine pulled out a small device from one of those pockets, Tourmaline felt that twinge spread all the way up into her legs.

Celandine reached out with the device but George grabbed her arm.

Tourmaline took him by the shoulders. "George, there's no time. I know it's scary, but we *have* to."

George swallowed. "I know. I think it's just a reflex at this point," he said.

Celandine slotted the device into a brass control panel on the wall, and the door glided open to reveal a long gallery.

"It worked!" said Mai. "Where did you get it?" The delight in her voice was so obvious that Tourmaline stepped inside the room before Celandine answered.

It didn't stop her hearing the other girl's answer, though. "I saw it on someone's desk and I thought we might need it, so I swiped it."

Tourmaline glanced over her shoulder. Mai was looking at Celandine in open admiration.

Tourmaline scowled. "What else have you done that we don't know about?"

Celandine's expression dipped into wariness for just

a second before it turned blank. Tourmaline looked to George and Mai to see if they'd noticed it too, but both of her friends were frowning at her.

She turned away.

In front of her, lining the gallery, were several larger magical artefacts spaced at intervals along the length of the room. Wood panelling covered the walls. There was a length of tapestried carpet running along the middle of the wooden parquet flooring and a slight mustiness in the air that suggested no one visited very often.

"This could be the right place," said Mai.

"Well, if it is, which one of these magical artefacts is causing the nothing?" asked George.

First, there was a silver suit of armour with a shining helmet and a drawn sword. Further along, a painting taller than Tourmaline hung on the wall. She tilted her head at the picture – which was of a ship not unlike *The Hunter* climbing a wave on a storm-tossed sea.

"It's not very good, is it?" she said.

"Terrible," Celandine agreed. "But is it the magical artefact that's making things disappear?"

Tourmaline looked round and realized that everyone

was waiting for her pronouncement.

She glanced at Celandine and lifted her chin. "I need to look at them all first." She moved down the gallery, almost certain that a good idea – which she didn't currently have – would occur to her.

After the painting, there was a long and beautiful dress on a tailor's dummy. It was an old-fashioned garment, with very wide skirts and many layers. Tourmaline looked at it with disdain. Even if it was a magical artefact, you could never climb rigging, or run full pelt down a cobbled street to escape a disgruntled adult wearing such a garment.

She passed on quickly to the next magical artefact, which was a chair. A perfectly ordinary-looking straight-backed chair, unremarkable in every way and, in fact, a little bit scratched.

"Is that a magical artefact?" asked Mai. "Or just ... a chair?"

"Let's assume it's a magical artefact and not sit in it," said George. "In case it does something unexpected."

Mai mused on this. "What if it's an eject seat, like on a small aeroplane? Or a musical chair, or a—"

But Tourmaline had already moved on to the next, and final, magical artefact. It was a child's tricycle, painted red with white wheels.

"So, which one could it be?" asked Mai, who was slightly wounded that no one ever wanted to listen to her third option when it came to the possibilities she saw in any given situation.

Tourmaline looked back down the line. "A trike, a chair, a dress, a painting and a suit of armour," she said.

They all looked down the length of the room. And then, suddenly, the chair wasn't there any more. Along with the surrounding carpet and wall, it was gone, replaced by a square and weighty chunk of nothing.

George looked at the ceiling and then warily all around. It wasn't getting any easier to accept.

Tourmaline started walking slowly backwards, staying away from the magical artefacts.

"It's OK if you don't know which one it is," said Celandine. "It's not like any of the rest of us know."

"She's right, Tourmaline," said George. "We really

don't know what to do. None of these things look like they're doing anything."

Tourmaline allowed a small, grateful smile on to her face and for once didn't mind that George was agreeing with Celandine.

"Perhaps," said Celandine, her mischievous eyebrows rising, "you should just try using one of them and see what happens?"

"I like that idea," said Tourmaline, who had had quite enough of thinking and not acting.

She reached out for the closest magical artefact, which was the oil painting.

"Tourmaline!" George grabbed her arm and held it tight.

"I'm only going to touch it," said Tourmaline. "I might be able to tell if this is the right artefact if I do."

"It probably is," said Celandine. "I don't see how a dress or a tricycle could make things disappear, do you?"

"I don't know," said Tourmaline. "That's why I was going to touch it."

George had not let go of her arm. "But if you do and

it *is* this magical artefact that's making things blink out of existence, what if you make it worse?"

Tourmaline gave him a look and George tucked his chin in. "I mean, not worse, but more. What if you amplify it like you do with magical artefacts and it makes even more things disappear? Or it does it faster, or the nothingness is bigger?"

Tourmaline's arm dropped to her side. "I'm glad you thought of that, George."

Mai was frowning at the remaining items in the room. "I don't know why any of these things would turn other things into no-things," she said. "Usually with magical artefacts, the magic matches the magical thing. But I don't see how a suit of armour or a painting matches up with turning everything into emptiness."

Celandine let out a lengthy sigh and turned away. "Maybe we're in the wrong place and we can't do anything and we're all going to be vanished into nowhere and so is my—"

She stopped suddenly and guiltily.

"So is your what?" asked Tourmaline, her voice accusing and suspicious.

"I saw a magical artefact I wanted in the museum," said Celandine. "I know it's not mine, but I – I was going to take it on the way out without anyone knowing."

This was perfectly understandable – Tourmaline had considered doing the very same thing herself. She just wasn't sure she entirely believed Celandine. The girl was a good liar but so was Tourmaline, which was why she recognized a lie when she heard one.

She stared at Celandine for a few seconds.

"Maybe it isn't one of these things at all," said George. The sleeves of his stolen jumper were in tatters at this point. "A painting of a ship and the sea has nothing to do with things disappearing, no matter how I think about it."

"Neither does a dress or a suit of armour," said Mai.

"Or a tricycle," said Celandine.

"It's a puzzle," said Tourmaline, almost to herself. "A puzzle that doesn't make the usual kind of sense. But it makes the magical kind of sense. Like everything did when we were on Elsewhere."

She suddenly sat on the floor, tenting her fingers

under her chin. Then she lay on the floor, scooted round until her head was facing the magical artefacts and tilted it until she was looking at them upside down.

Mai and George looked at each other in alarm.

"Tourmaline? Are you all right?" asked Mai.

"I'm just trying to look at things differently," she said. This might have been a little more literal than most people would have deemed necessary, but in this case, it worked for Tourmaline.

She scrambled upright, leaving a wet patch of carpet where she had been lying. "What is a suit of armour for?"

Celandine shrugged. "For fighting. In battles."

"No," said Tourmaline. "I mean, yes, but it doesn't *help* with the fighting part, does it?"

"It helps with the not-getting-your-arms-chopped-off bit," said Mai.

Tourmaline smiled. "Exactly."

"It's a defence!" said George, suddenly getting excited.

"Yes," said Tourmaline. "Like on the island of Elsewhere."

"That makes sense!" said Mai. "Magic always wants to protect itself."

"So ... this is the museum's defence?" asked Celandine. "A sort of defence against intruders. To stop magical artefacts getting into the wrong hands."

"Yes!" said George. "It's making them disappear instead. And we're the ones who set it off."

"Trying to take the things from Captain Violet's list!" said Mai.

"But it's not stopping, and it's going to take all of AICMA headquarters," said Tourmaline. "I'm right, aren't I?"

George nodded. "This is the magical artefact causing the nothing."

"Brilliant! Now how do we stop it?" asked Mai. She looked at Tourmaline.

They *all* looked at Tourmaline.

Tourmaline's face fell. She shook her head.

She didn't know.

Chapter
Twenty-three

Once upon a time, if Tourmaline didn't know how to do something, she would have tried several increasingly desperate ways and just kept going until she got lucky.

She would probably still do that, now and again, for the rest of her life. It was just a very Tourmaline-ish thing to do. But right then, she made herself stop and think. Which was a much more George-ish thing to do. It was a strategy she had noticed worked and she had been trying to incorporate it more into the way she went about tackling problems. She didn't count nearly touching a possibly dangerous magical artefact just a few minutes ago – she was still Tourmaline, after all.

"Well," she said slowly. "We can't trick it into thinking the museum is safe by putting everything back where it was, because a lot of things are gone now. And if we bring the octopus back, which we wouldn't ever do, there's going to be nowhere to put it. So if we can't bring things back we have to..." She paused and screwed her eyes up tight for a second to help with the slower thinking. "We have to take things out."

"What do you mean?" asked Celandine.

"Take the suit of armour out of the building," said Tourmaline.

"And you think that will stop it?" asked George.

"I think so," said Tourmaline. "It wants to defend, so if it's outside in the nice calm clearing with nothing to protect, it will stop. At least, it probably will."

"I really hope you're right," said Celandine. She lifted her chin to the space where the oil painting had been.

"I am," said Tourmaline. That was quite enough slow thinking and she was ready for some fast acting.

Mai was looking up at the armour. "How?"

"What?" asked Tourmaline.

"*How* are we supposed to get it out of here? It's huge. And it looked heavy. *And* you can't touch it, in case you make it wor— I mean, more."

"The rest of us will have to do it," said George.

"What if it makes *us* disappear?" asked Mai.

But George was already shaking his head. He pointed out that if the suit was defending the museum from marauders it would hardly vanish itself. After that, everyone except Tourmaline felt a bit better.

He took a deep breath and a long look at Tourmaline to remind himself that he trusted her more than anyone, and then pulled at the arm of the armour. There was a heavy, plated glove, and several larger plates, jointed at the elbow.

Nothing happened.

Mai moved him out of the way and yanked the arm straight off.

Celandine scrambled up the torso of the suit and plucked the helmet off the body.

After a few minutes' work, Celandine was wearing the helmet and a breastplate that went down to her knees. Mai had two arms and two legs covering her own two arms and legs, and George was dragging a heavy sword that was taller than he was as they left the gallery.

Tourmaline, who was wishing she could have worn a

bit of the armour, consoled herself by leading the way and telling herself that it had been her idea in the first place.

Mai clanked along behind her and George's sword scraped the floor and clanged up the steps. The visor on the helmet kept falling into Celandine's eyes, making her bump into walls.

Alarming patches of nothing appeared, but they hurried on.

When they reached the curator, the woman put down the papers she had been tidying and lifted up her spectacles so that she could take in the full effect.

The filing cabinet next to her promptly disappeared, and George gave her an apologetic smile before rushing off after the others to the door.

"I hope this works," he said to Tourmaline. "Otherwise the magic might disappear the whole of the AICMA headquarters."

"Don't worry," said Tourmaline, who was herself actually quite worried. "This is definitely going to work." She led the way out of the building, into a very bright early autumn afternoon. Everyone blinked and felt strange when they remembered the world outside was real and all in one piece.

"Oh, that's better," said George, dragging the sword a final few metres away from the AICMA headquarters and dropping it in the grass. Mai let the armour arms fall and kicked off the boots and legs. She helped Celandine out of the breastplate. Celandine threw the helmet down and scrubbed her hands through her pixie hair.

"What now?" asked Mai, as they surveyed the jumbled armour piled in the peaceful clearing.

"Now we go back in – it will be safe," said Tourmaline. "We find the postcard sender and we finally figure out *everything* about my magic." She squeezed some of the water out of her trousers on to the grass.

"Then we all go home, eat quite a lot and live happily ever after," said George hopefully.

"Yes. That," said Tourmaline.

"The crew are coming," said Mai.

The captain strode out of the treeline, the gold buttons on her jacket flashing in the sun.

"Is the octopus OK?" Mai called.

"Back in the sea where she belongs," said Quintalle gruffly.

The captain looked down at the armour. "I don't think this was on our list," she said, raising her eyebrows at Miracle, who shook her head.

"But we'll take it," said Dexta, reaching for the helmet.

Tourmaline neatly slapped her hand away and there was a tense minute where knives were drawn (Dexta), threats were made (Quintalle), apologies were offered (George), and an explanation offered for why the suit of armour must be left alone and why it would no longer be possible to get the items from the captain's list because they had mostly disappeared (Tourmaline).

The captain listened carefully. And when Tourmaline had finished, she nodded.

"I understand perfectly why we can no longer have the magical artefacts we would very much have liked," she said.

"Good," said Tourmaline.

"However," said the captain. "I'm sure that *you* understand perfectly why we no longer have an agreement whereby I turn a blind eye and let the reward money for capturing you go to someone else."

"What?" said Tourmaline.

"It's nothing personal," said the captain. "It's just that business is business."

"But we have to rescue the curator and ... anyone else in the building!" said Tourmaline.

"From what you just told me about the armour, anyone inside the AICMA headquarters is quite safe now," said Captain Violet.

"Not that we care about anyone who works for the AICMA," said Miracle.

"But we had a deal!" said George in outrage.

"Which you broke," said Dexta.

"But that's not our fault," said Mai.

"We don't much care," said Quintalle.

"You could take the airship instead," said Tourmaline suddenly. "Instead of me. It's magical and probably worth a fortune and if you don't want to sell it then you could keep it."

Captain Violet looked thoughtful. She glanced at each of the crew and an unspoken conversation took place.

"We think," said the captain, "that is an excellent idea."

Dexta casually walked round behind the children, just as casually tossing one of her flashing knives end over end. Celandine narrowed her eyes at the blue-haired hunter.

"We'll take both," said Captain Violet, giving Dexta a nod.

Suddenly the pointy end of Dexta's knife was very close to the squishy part on the back of George's arm. He let out a squeak.

Tourmaline scowled her deepest scowl at the captain.

"Oh, don't be like that, Tourmaline. You'll easily be able to escape from Winona. Feel free to do so as soon as we have our money. In fact, if I'm feeling generous, we might even give you a helping hand. The money's the important part, you see." She stopped and tilted her head. "I wonder if we'll get extra since there are four of you."

Dexta prodded George and they headed towards the airship.

"You can't really blame us," the captain continued as they boarded. "You owe us *something*. Because I can't remember where the island of Elsewhere is and neither can the crew, and to be honest none of us are very happy about it."

Tourmaline heard a low growl behind her and spun round to see Quintalle Nix glowering at her. Since Tourmaline had been the one to make the captain forget the location of the island, she decided to change the subject quickly. "What do you think of the ship?"

Captain Violet looked around. "She's a beauty."

The crew were rifling through the bunks and exclaiming over the controls. Dexta had closed the doors but was keeping one eye on the children and a shiny knife to hand.

"To the Dark Market!" said Miracle.

"And our reward!" added Dexta.

Tourmaline crossed her arms and shot vicious looks at all of them, which made the captain and Quintalle cackle, which then made Tourmaline furious.

As the crew turned away from her and started to discuss flying the airship and handing over Tourmaline in such a way that they didn't get tricked or swindled, Tourmaline turned to her own crew.

"Ideas?" she asked.

"There's four of us and four of them," said Celandine. "I reckon we should fight."

George, who had a wary eye on Dexta's knife, looked at Tourmaline in alarm.

"I don't think that's very practical," said Tourmaline. "Especially for you, since you're very small."

"But I'm fierce," said Celandine indignantly. "And you're not much bigger than I am, anyway."

Mai let out a sharp breath and folded her arms. "I'm the biggest and the crew are *all* bigger than me. We can't fight." She sounded slightly sad about it.

"Maybe they won't be able to figure out how to fly the ship," said George.

The airship shot up into the air, and George stumbled into Mai, who set him straight. He shrugged at Tourmaline helplessly.

Tourmaline closed her eyes briefly. When she opened them, the ground was far below and her hopes had been left behind with it. Out of the porthole, she could see the clearing and the discarded armour shining in the sunlight.

She had been so very close to discovering it all – the

mysterious postcard sender had been *right there* waiting for her, ready to tell her everything she needed to know about controlling her magic.

Now she was a prisoner, heading back to the Dark Market and the woman who wanted to lock her up and use her magic for her own selfish gain.

Chapter
Twenty-four

"I did a much better job of sailing this ship," Mai muttered as the crew poked and pulled at the controls and the airship lurched away from the Museum of Marvels and Tourmaline's chance to find out who had been sending her the postcards.

Tourmaline opened her mouth, either to complain to her friends or to try to persuade the captain not to kidnap her – she wasn't sure which – when the airship suddenly dropped. Her feet left the floor and the words left her head.

She jolted back down, tumbling into Mai and George. Celandine had managed to stay on her feet. Suddenly the crew were shouting. The captain was yelling orders, Dexta was grasping her knives tightly,

Miracle and Quintalle were craning their necks to scan the sky out of the large front window.

Tourmaline ran to the nearest porthole. Something knocked into the side of the ship and she banged her head on the small window.

"What's happening?" asked George, clinging to a bunk.

Tourmaline rubbed her head and braced herself, then looked out into the sky. She was just about to answer that she couldn't see anything, when she caught a glimpse of something that was half hidden by clouds. Something large and brown and impossible. She ran to the next porthole and Mai and Celandine took the one she had just been using.

"What *is* that?" asked Mai.

Tourmaline pressed her face to the small circle of glass. There it was again, a snatch of something that couldn't be in the sky. She looked down to the ground, but they were definitely still in the air, Escea below them clipping by at pace.

When she looked back up, the impossible thing was visible in a patch of clear sky. Tourmaline sucked in a breath of wonder. It was a ship – an actual ship, made for the sea, but scudding through the sky. Wooden oars protruded from holes in its sides, propelling it in the air. On its prow there was a carved figure – half woman, half fish – and on its side *The Mermaid* was painted in black lettering. The ship's sails were a dark, russet red to match the carved mermaid's hair.

"It's a ship!" Tourmaline called out.

"What's its name?" asked Miracle, running from the captain's side to look.

"*The Mermaid*," said Celandine.

Miracle pushed Tourmaline out of the way and her black eyes went wide. "We're under attack!"

George made a noise of alarm. "Why are they attacking us?"

Quintalle scowled at Tourmaline. "There's a big reward on her head."

Tourmaline scowled right back. "This wouldn't be happening if you hadn't stolen me to start with!"

"Is it rogue hunters?" asked George. His fingers, still clinging to the bunk, were blanched white.

The captain turned around, looking grim. "Word is

out about you, Tourmaline Grey. It looks like we've got competition."

"Well, *do* something!" Mai demanded. "We can't let them get Tourmaline."

"I completely agree, believe me," said the captain, in a way that didn't seem as though it was about the reward (or at least not entirely).

"Are they – are they very bad?" asked George, trying to see out of a porthole without letting go of the bunk. The crew looked worried. And the crew *never* looked worried – even about things that George wasn't sure were right or wrong, only that they weren't fully either. It wasn't reassuring.

"That depends on what you think is bad," said Captain Violet.

"But they're a *lot* worse than us," said Dexta.

Suddenly there was a loud bang and a puff of smoke from the side of *The Mermaid*.

Tourmaline frowned as something black and round came hurtling through the air towards her.

"Cannon!" shouted Quintalle.

The captain hauled on the wheel, the airship turned

at the last second and the cannonball sailed past. Tourmaline ran to the other side of the airship and watched as it landed in a lake below, causing the most spectacular splash and startling a flock of geese who had been swimming around minding their own business.

"Just a warning shot," yelled the captain.

"Warning us about what?" asked George, sounding as though he didn't much want to know the answer.

"What they'll do to us if we don't hand Tourmaline over, I should think," the captain answered.

"Do you think we should treat with them?" Quintalle asked. Her customary scowl was on her face, but her gaze kept darting out of the window.

"You can't make a deal to hand Tourmaline over!" said George.

The Mermaid sailed closer, looming through the clouds, easily keeping pace with the little airship.

"I won't go," said Tourmaline. It seemed far better to stay with the rogue hunters she knew than go with the fearsome-looking rogue hunters she didn't. "They can't make me."

"Except they can," said Miracle.

"Just like we did," said Dexta.

On the other ship, there was now a crew above deck.

"They want to talk, Captain," said Quintalle.

The captain threw some levers and the airship came to a bumpy stop. *The Mermaid* sailed closer until they were alongside and Tourmaline could see the other crew clearly.

George carefully pattered over to look too. Five women and one man stood on the deck, all dressed in black and burgundy, the colours of *The Mermaid*. They had an array of weapons, from cutlasses to throwing stars to axes. Their captain was younger than Captain Violet and much larger. Her black hair ran in braids from under her black hat and her boots were tall and scuffed.

When she held her hand up, she was missing two fingers.

"Open the porthole," Captain Violet ordered. Quintalle unfastened one of the small round windows, and Captain Violet drew herself up to her full height and stood in front of it.

"Captain Violet!" the other captain shouted across.

"I thought from the terrible sailing that it was you."

"Captain Belvedere!" Violet bellowed back. "I saw from your inferior vessel that it was you."

Behind Belvedere, several of her crew drew their weapons. "Hand over the girl and we *might* not blow you out of the sky."

Tourmaline wrestled her own porthole open. "My *name* is Tourmaline Grey and I'm not going anywhere with you!"

Miracle stepped to Captain Violet's side and said quietly into her ear, "They've got their hands on a pretty powerful magical artefact there. I'd heard the rumours about what *The Mermaid* can do but I didn't quite believe it until now. I don't think we can outrun them, Captain."

"Then we'll fight them," said Quintalle fiercely.

"What if they blow a hole in the balloon silk?" asked George.

Tourmaline imagined plummeting to the ground like a popped birthday balloon, only with a far less comical ending.

"I'm not scared of them," growled Quintalle.

"Bunch of fancy-shirt-wearing muzzy bilge rats."

Captain Violet turned to Tourmaline. "What weapons does this vessel have?" she asked.

Tourmaline shook her head. "None."

There was a stunned silence. The crew all looked puzzled.

"Defences, then," said the captain. "What defences does it have?"

"Nothing!" said Tourmaline. "It belongs to a university. My mother borrowed it and it's for – for travelling. Not for blowing things up."

The crew exchanged baffled glances.

"How do you fend off marauders who want to steal your haul?" asked Quintalle.

"We *don't*," said George. "We don't have a haul. Or marauders."

"What a strange way to live," said Dexta.

"Well, in any case, that settles it," said Captain Violet. "We can't attack them and we can't defend ourselves, so we don't have any other choice."

"What does that mean?" asked Tourmaline suspiciously.

The captain shrugged. "We'll just *have* to outrun them."

Tourmaline smiled.

Mai strode forwards to the controls. "In that case," she said, "I'd better sail the ship."

"I agree," said Tourmaline. "She's much better at it than any of you."

"I'm not going to wait forever for an answer!" Captain Belvedere shouted.

"You can do what you like," yelled Captain Violet. "But you'll have to catch us first!"

She made a very rude gesture at the other captain. Mai threw two levers all the way down and grabbed the wheel. The airship shot off across Escea before the shocked look on George's face had even faded.

Behind them, an enraged roar from Captain Belvedere tapered off into the sky.

Captain Violet cackled and the crew joined in, Dexta clapping Mai on the back so hard she almost fell over.

Tourmaline craned her neck to look back out of the porthole.

"Are they following us?" asked George.

"Yes." The other ship was sailing through the air, long, powerful pulls on the oars aided by the wind in its burgundy sails. She looked down. They were flying out over the coast, cliffs dropping suddenly to a choppy ocean. Dark shapes and shadows moved under the water.

"They're gaining on us," Dexta called out.

"If they pull alongside us, they'll fire again," said Captain Violet.

Mai tried to push the levers down more, but they had already gone as far as they could. The airship couldn't go any faster.

The Mermaid drew closer. Captain Belvedere stood at the prow. Before, she had looked furious, but now she was grinning as they gained on the airship.

"Mai!" said Tourmaline.

"She can't go any faster!" said Mai.

The Mermaid pulled even with the airship, so close Tourmaline could see the look of triumph on Captain Belvedere's face. There was something familiar about the expression, but before Tourmaline could think about it she noticed something happening below deck. Several hatches in the side of the ship opened as the oars arced through the air.

"You'd better think of something," said Quintalle darkly. "They're priming every cannon they have."

Chapter
Twenty-five

"She really won't go any faster," Mai said, throwing an anguished glance back at her friends.

"Then don't go faster," said George, suddenly standing up from his place clinging to the bunk. "Go down," he said. "Dive!"

"Hurry!" said Tourmaline.

The thunder of the cannons going off in unison sounded just as Mai threw all the controls down. The airship dropped at a steep angle. Celandine, George and Tourmaline clung on for dear life (George's eyes were closed), and the cannonballs sailed overhead, crashing into the ocean and sending a fountain of white foam into the air.

The airship levelled out as Mai took it down so low it

skimmed the waves, sea spray flying up to drum on the front window and speckle the portholes.

"Good sailing," said Captain Violet approvingly and even Quintalle grunted her agreement. "But we can't outmanoeuvre them forever. We need a plan. What do you think, George?"

George looked startled, then extremely pleased to have been asked, then a bit dismayed. "I don't know," he admitted.

"We're flying over land again," said Mai, sailing back up and up and up. It was a mountain range – jagged rocks and snow-capped peaks with deep rifts between them.

Dexta ran to each of the portholes in turn, her blue hair flashing past. "They're gaining ground!"

"I've got an idea," said Mai. "Maybe we can lose them."

She veered wildly to the right and Tourmaline slid across the floor to George. The airship had dropped into a crevice, the light inside it dimming as the porthole views filled with craggy rock.

"Good idea, Mai," said Dexta. "They can't follow us

down here, *The Mermaid* is too big to fit."

Mai let out a big breath and slowed the ship down so she could navigate the path between the mountains. Tourmaline came to stand beside her and after a few moments of reduced speed and steady sailing, even George ventured forwards to see. Ahead of them, the mountain range seemed to go on forever. The peaks soared upwards until they disappeared into the clouds. Snow covered the sides and caps in great patches of undisturbed white.

Fresh mountain air came in through the open portholes, smelling like snow and exploring. Tourmaline pointed out of the window – a family of spotted snow foxes were frolicking below, powdery crystals shooting up under their paws as they jumped and landed. George nudged Tourmaline and pointed too – at a winter hare, still and hiding on a ledge close by.

"It's beautiful," said Celandine in a hushed whisper. She was standing behind Tourmaline and George, on her tiptoes so she could see between their shoulders.

The cold sky above was a brilliant blue, and despite the crew of *The Mermaid* trying to steal Tourmaline from the crew of *The Hunter*, who had already stolen her, her heart soared like the ice eagle that was wheeling and arcing in the sky above the fox pups.

Tourmaline turned to smile at Celandine – a big, open, uplifted smile. This was what she was made for – a wild adventure, friends at her side, danger all around and the wide world in front of her.

"This is the life!" said Quintalle, and her face cracked into a startling smile. Tourmaline couldn't have agreed more.

"Although it might end more quickly than we'd all probably like if we aren't careful," said Dexta, pointing further ahead. Aboard *The Hunter* she could often be found in the crow's nest, looking out for land or trouble or treasure. The airship didn't exactly have a crow's nest, so she'd clambered on to a top bunk and was crouched there squinting into the distance.

Ahead of the airship, the mountain pass they were cruising through narrowed to a jagged slit of rock.

"Go up," said George, grabbing Mai's arm.

"She can't," said Captain Violet, leaning into the window, her eyes lifted to the sky. "*The Mermaid* is right above us. They're running us into the ground."

The rocks loomed closer.

"I can make it!" Mai said, a look of concentration on her face.

The crew started running around, closing the portholes, yelling at each other about fighting the other crew, but Captain Violet held out both arms to still them. Everyone held their breath as Mai reached the first jutting rock and gingerly steered round it. George looked at Tourmaline instead of out of the window so he could still see how bad it was from her face, but not *exactly* how bad.

"That's it, Mai," Celandine muttered as the rocks closed in around them, pointing jagged, accusatory fingers.

The mountains squeezed together and it went quite dark in the airship, almost as though they were underwater. The frown of concentration on Mai's face was ferocious. The airship glided forwards as black rock skimmed the glass of the portholes.

Then the sides of the ship made contact and a scraping sound echoed in the mountain air. It felt a bit like being inside a pepper grinder and was astoundingly loud.

"Easy does it," Miracle murmured from behind the captain.

"She can do it," said Dexta.

"Of course she can," said Tourmaline stoutly. Snow was landing in clotted clumps on the roof of the ship. Its sides were being shaved and peeled by the mountains. But Tourmaline had faith in her friend.

Mai inched through the rift, little by little. The airship held. And after far too long, the mountain passage opened up and they sailed into a canyon that lay between two peaks.

"Well done, Captain Cravenswood," said Captain Violet. The crew set about cheering and whooping and clapping Mai on the back. Even George managed a small, still mildly terrified smile.

"You were brilliant," said Tourmaline.

"Absolutely brilliant," said Celandine.

But George had a listening expression on his face.

"What's the matter?" asked Tourmaline.

"I can hear something." He held a hand up and the crew all stilled. Dexta pulled out a couple of knives and

Quintalle resumed her customary scowl in case battle was imminent.

"I can't hear anything," said Captain Violet.

"I can," said Tourmaline. "It's a ... hissing."

"It – it sounds like air," said George, worry spreading all over his face. "Air escaping."

Tourmaline ran to a porthole, opened it and looked up.

The silk above – which was now a patchwork of white and blue and black to reflect the snow, sky and rocks – was sagging to one side.

The airship's balloon had punctured.

Chapter
Twenty-six

"We're sinking!" said Tourmaline.

Mai looked utterly dejected so George went and stood right next to her.

"It's not your fault, Mai," said Tourmaline. "You're the best at flying. It's the stupid rocks' fault."

"What are we going to do?" said George, staring down at the looming ground. "We can't get trapped in these mountains. We're in the middle of nowhere." He looked down at the shorts he was wearing. "We'll freeze."

"Unless Captain Belvedere and her crew get their hands on us," said Miracle. "Then we'll probably expire a whole lot quicker."

George didn't look at all reassured by this.

Tourmaline suddenly made a noise. A noise that said she'd thought of something and she couldn't believe she hadn't thought of it before. "No!" she said. "We're not going to freeze or starve or anything else." (She was getting quite hungry.)

Everyone looked at her.

"Magic!" she said. "I'm magic and I can *use* it!"

At that moment, something hit the top of the airship and knocked it down another few feet towards the ground.

"It's a rope," said Celandine, sticking her head out of a porthole. "And the crew of *The Mermaid* are climbing down it."

"Prepare to be boarded," said Captain Violet, a dangerous glint in her eye.

"No," said Tourmaline. "I don't think I will."

She dashed over to the controls of the airship. "Mai?"

Mai took the controls. Tourmaline put her hands on the dashboard and tried very hard to think only about the airship and about flying and about escaping and *not* about being captured by someone much worse than Captain Violet.

There were shouts outside and thumps on the roof. The airship tilted to one side and then the other. The ground was getting closer.

"Don't think about them," George whispered. "Think about the magic."

And Tourmaline did. She thought so hard about it that it made her sweat a little bit.

There was a bump under her feet and a crunching sound – the airship had hit the ground.

Tourmaline screwed her eyes up tight. Her fingers pressed into the wood and brass controls and she wished and hoped and thought furiously about magic. About making the airship more, and about escaping. George gave a little squeak and she cracked one eye open. Her hands were glowing, making the brass controls shine. The airship jumped up into the air and a member of Captain Belvedere's crew slid past the front window, a look of surprise on her face. The airship continued to rise and the shouts outside became less fierce and more startled.

Then suddenly the airship shot off, magic buoying it into the air and forwards. George slid back along the floor and Mai gripped the controls tightly.

"Ha!" Quintalle grinned and pointed out of the back door. Captain Belvedere and her crew were clinging to their ropes in mid-air, dangling below *The Mermaid*.

The airship soared up and away leaving Captain Belvedere roaring with anger and Captain Violet roaring with delight.

"Look at what our Tourmaline can do!" she crowed.

Mai was piloting the airship past craggy outcrops and rocky ledges as it got faster and faster and finally shot up past the highest mountain peak and into the clouds. "They'll never catch us now!" she cried.

"Maybe we could slow down, just a bit, then," said George. They were whipping past clouds and startled birds faster than *The Hunter* had sailed the seas, faster than the stolen motorcycle to Brenia port, faster even than the zipline on Somewhere.

"I say go faster," said Dexta. She opened a porthole and her short blue hair streamed backwards as the wind ripped through it. The crew were enjoying themselves enormously.

"Imagine *The Hunter* going this fast!" said Miracle.

"Imagine," said Tourmaline, "if we *didn't* go to the Dark Market, and *instead* you let me go back to the Museum of Marvels where I need to be right now?"

The crew were quiet. They looked at Captain Violet.

The captain thought. A crafty look crossed her face and her blue eyes gleamed. "I think we can come to an arrangement, Tourmaline Grey."

"An arrangement where we go straight back to the AICMA headquarters?"

"An arrangement where you, a magical girl, owe us, your good friends, a large and to-be-decided-on favour."

Tourmaline sighed. It was only to be expected from rogue hunters, from Captain Violet in particular, but after everything she'd already had to put up with it was a bit much to owe someone a favour for *not* kidnapping her.

"What about Winona, Captain?" asked Miracle.

"I think having Tourmaline owe us might be worth more than Winona is offering," said the captain. "Do we have an agreement, Tourmaline?"

"I suppose so," she said, and gave George a wink. Right at that moment, speeding through the sky because of her very own magic, she had no intention of doing anything for Captain Violet.

"Excellent," said the captain. "Then set a course for the AICMA headquarters. I think the crew and I might be off to lie low for a little while after that."

"And maybe plot some revenge on *The Mermaid*," added Quintalle, sounding surly but hopeful.

"I like that idea very much, First Mate Nix," said the captain, and the crew retreated to the back of the ship to make a daring plan that involved a lot of stealing, some sinking and much walking of the plank.

Tourmaline cast a wary glance back and slipped the compass out of her pocket, opening it to whisper where they wanted to go. Mai turned the wheel and the airship curved round in a smooth arc as she adjusted course.

"Mai," said George. He motioned downwards and Mai saw what his eyebrows were begging her to do. They were very high up, and though Tourmaline's magic was wonderful and seemed determined to get them back to the museum as fast as possible, the ground being so very far away didn't seem ideal if any other calamities were to befall the airship.

Mai nudged the controls until the airship was only quite high, just above the tops of the trees. It had flown so fast with Tourmaline's magic helping it along that they would be back at the museum in no time. Mai recognized the lake below, and after that, the towns and farms and clock towers and shops.

George peered up through the porthole at the ragged balloon above them and then wished he hadn't. Tourmaline's magic had filled the balloon and made it work again, even better than before. But it hadn't completely fixed the jagged tear in the silk.

As he watched, though, the silk began to mend itself back together, the fabric melding until the balloon was as good as new and he could hardly believe there had been a rip with frayed edges there seconds before. The whole effect was incredible, but also mind-bending and precarious and George hastily closed the porthole. He looked at his friend in wonder for some time. It was down to Tourmaline that they were rapidly speeding along the coast of Escea and hovering near the AICMA headquarters.

Mai slowed and then stopped, somewhere above the forest and not quite at the clearing, the body of the airship nestled into the top of the trees so that only the balloon rose above the leaves.

The four children exchanged glances. The clearing was no longer empty. It was full of motorcars and motorcycles (and one bright red hang glider). It was also full of people. Not just people. *Agents*. AICMA agents everywhere.

Chapter
Twenty-seven

In the clearing, several agents were standing over the discarded suit of armour – one with a clipboard, one holding up various parts of the metal with a pair of tongs, and three more conducting a lively conversation that involved a lot of pointing back at where the headquarters building would be if it was visible.

"I hope they're not going to take it back inside," said Mai.

"I don't think they would," said George. "The curator must have told them what it was doing. They're probably just trying to figure out how it works."

"That's not even our biggest problem." Celandine threw up her hands in frustration and gestured at the scene below where agents were swarming all over the clearing and running in and out of the headquarters. It was a very strange effect – the building shimmering into view briefly as people came and went.

"No, it's not," said Tourmaline. "They're everywhere. We're so close to the postcard sender, I can't give up. But how am I going to get into the building now?"

"How are *we* going to get into the building now?" said George. He was feeling a lot braver since they'd stopped flying and there was a good chance they'd soon be back on the ground.

"I think," said Captain Violet from the back of the airship, "that we might be able to help you with that."

Tourmaline turned round in surprise. The captain smiled innocently, which instantly made her suspicious.

"Help us how?" she asked.

"We could distract all those agents so that you can sneak back in," said the captain.

"We're very good at that sort of thing," said Miracle. "Also, we're wanted by the AICMA, so it won't be hard to get them to chase after us."

"*Very* wanted," said Quintalle, and she laughed so loud she made herself cough.

"We'll get their attention," said the captain. "Keep close to the ground, and then when they're all following us, you can slip into the building while we sail off into the sky to new adventures."

"And heists," added Dexta.

"And a lot of stealing and thievery," added Miracle.

"All the good things," the captain promised.

The crew cheered. George frowned.

"But that would mean you get to keep the airship," said Tourmaline. She couldn't think of a better idea and had already decided to say yes but felt as though she shouldn't buckle immediately – if only to make George feel better.

"I suppose it would," said the captain, looking very much like she'd already thought of this and that it was exactly why she was suggesting that she help in the first place.

Tourmaline looked at her friends.

"I think we should do it," said Mai.

"What are we waiting for? Let's go!" said Celandine.

George gave an only slightly unhappy nod, so Tourmaline gave one too. "Deal," she said.

"Splendid," said Captain Violet.

Dexta threw open the back doors and kicked out the rope ladder. It dropped through the trees, the end of it coming to rest almost on the ground. She gestured to it as it dangled.

George's eyes widened. "Can't you land the ship?"

"Absolutely not," said the captain. "If we're caught, we'll end up in AICMA custody, and while I have no doubt we could escape, it would be inconvenient when we have so much else to do. Not to mention they would definitely confiscate this ship and certainly sink *The Hunter*."

"If they ever figure out where it is," added Quintalle.

"Although it's really not worth the risk," added Dexta.

"What about the risk to us?" asked George, his worries outweighing how intimidating he still found Captain Violet.

"I don't think they take children into custody," said the captain, shepherding them towards the rope ladder. "Especially if they don't get caught," she added, giving Tourmaline a significant look.

Several minutes and a few scratches and scuffs later, the children were on the ground.

Tourmaline looked up. Dexta was hanging out of the back of the airship looking quite at home and very pleased with herself.

"I hope Persephone won't be angry with us for giving the airship away," said George.

"Not if we explain properly," said Tourmaline.

"And if that doesn't work, we could just tell her that Captain Violet took it," said Mai. "Because there wasn't anything else we could do so it's almost the truth."

"We're ready!" Celandine called up in a whisper-shout.

Dexta gave a little salute and the doors promptly closed.

Celandine crept forwards to the treeline. Tourmaline followed, sped up and overtook her, which was only fair since this was her adventure.

"Do you think we can trust them?" asked George as he caught up. He glanced back at the airship and then out at the clearing, which was still full of agents.

Tourmaline gave him a look.

"I don't mean in general," said George. "I just mean right now."

At that moment, the airship glided smoothly forwards (Captain Violet had obviously been watching how Mai piloted). The portholes opened and objects started raining down.

A fountain pen plummeted from the sky to plunge straight into the ground like a tiny javelin, right next to a startled agent. Teacups and spoons, the jar that had once contained an octopus (now safely in the sea thanks to Quintalle). Anything that wasn't nailed down, the crew threw out of the windows.

"What—?" spluttered one of the agents.

"Who is that?" another agent asked loudly.

Suddenly they were all were gathered together, looking upwards. One woman opened an umbrella as a collection of coins plummeted from the airship.

"Now!" cried Tourmaline, launching herself out of the trees and across the clearing. Celandine was right on her heels, followed by Mai and George, who did a

302

crouch-run, hoping to make himself and what was left of his stripey jumper less noticeable.

The agents were so outraged at the undignified treatment from the crew that not one of them saw.

"Is that...? I've seen a picture of that woman before," an agent said.

"It's – it's Captain Violet and the crew of *The Hunter*!" the lady under the umbrella declared. She sounded absolutely scandalized.

The crew were running out of objects to throw and were now hurling insults out of the windows instead as the airship dipped lower and then slowly started to move away from the headquarters.

"Apprehend those rogue hunters!" shouted an agent, her face red with outrage.

"You couldn't catch a one-legged crab in a rockpool!" Quintalle yelled out of a porthole. She threw what looked like a very hard bread roll for good measure and it hit the woman, causing quite a stir of indignation. The agents broke apart from their clump, some scurrying for their motorcars, some running for motorcycles, one intrepid woman even wrestling with the red hang glider.

No one looked at the children as Tourmaline stormed up to the door of the museum.

"This way!" Celandine beckoned them wildly. She ran over to a different door. "Come on! Hurry up!"

Tourmaline paused and Mai ran into the back of her, bundling her along. There wasn't time to question Celandine, even though Tourmaline's first instinct was to do exactly that – Celandine had already tugged the bell pull. The portcullis rattled up, the noise covered by the engines starting and motorcycles revving as they tore out of the clearing and into the forest in pursuit of the airship.

Celandine pulled open the door – fortunately left unlocked by the agents earlier – and ushered everyone inside.

Tourmaline resisted the ushering.

"I'm just trying to help!" said Celandine. "You don't want to get caught, do you?"

Tourmaline glanced over her shoulder. The last of the motorcars was leaving the clearing in a cloud of smoke but there could be other agents inside. They would have to be very careful. And very fast. She stepped inside quickly, but not before she saw the sign outside the door.

It said **Containment**.

Chapter
Twenty-eight

"Why did you choose Containment?" asked Tourmaline. They were inside and, unlike the museum, it was a small space – more of a corridor really, with a very large and very strange door at the other end. The door from the postcard.

Celandine shrugged as though it were obvious. "Because of the card you got," she said.

Tourmaline pulled out the postcard from her pocket. It hadn't been that long since she'd got it but given how much had happened, it *felt* as though it had been a very long time indeed. The card was creased and the ink was smeared and it looked as though it had been through a lot, which was how Tourmaline felt. She read it out loud:

I've helped you for free,
Now will you help me?
The thing I most need,
Is to be truly freed.

Your turn, Tourmaline.

"See," said Celandine. "It makes sense, doesn't it? Containment. Where things, or people, are contained. And this is the right door."

"I know what containment is," said Tourmaline, and she thrust the postcard back into her pocket and strode to the end of the corridor to the very large and very strange door.

"Open it," said Celandine. "With the magic key!" She was slotting her fingers together and pulling them apart, an eager, wary look on her face.

Tourmaline crossed her arms. "First, I want to know why you care so much about this. The postcards were addressed to *me*."

"Yes, but we all care," said George, giving Celandine a kind little smile.

"That's right," said Celandine. "Maybe we haven't known each other long but we're friends, aren't we? I *did* get Persephone back into the Dark Market. And the thing with the octopus that we did together. Not a lot of people can say they saved an octopus from the AICMA headquarters and gave it to a rogue hunter so she could set it free."

Mai shrugged. "I suspect *nobody* else could say that."

Celandine smiled at Tourmaline and Tourmaline found herself smiling back only slightly begrudgingly. "OK," she said. "But I can't open the door with the key. Look. It needs *three* keys."

The door was wide and high and the face of it was covered in a complicated metal mechanism with interlinked cogs and levers. At either side there were two keyholes and at the top, higher than even Mai could reach, was another.

"I bet they all have to be turned at the same time," said George.

"If we even had three keys," said Tourmaline, "which we don't."

It was a very imposing door. George shook his head.

"This is the kind of door that looks like it shouldn't be opened lightly," he said. "Do you know what I mean?"

"It's not very comforting, is it?" said Mai. "The AICMA must really have wanted to lock away whatever's behind it."

"And for it not to get out," added George.

"What are you saying?" asked Tourmaline.

"Just that we should think about this first," said George.

Tourmaline crossed her arms. "I *have* thought about it. I've been thinking about who sent the postcards since I got the first one. I've been thinking about my magic ever since I fell into the Source and that was *weeks* ago."

"I know," said George gently. "It's a lot of thinking."

"George is right, though," said Mai. "What if it's someone really bad in there? Or some*thing* really bad?" Mai was clearly gearing up to present several terrible possibilities, so George quickly stepped in.

"The point is," he said, "we don't know what this person will do once we open the door. We've been captured a *lot* recently."

He looked quite tired and his jumper sleeves

were in shreds. Tourmaline patted his arm. "I know. There has been a lot of capturing. But I won't let that happen again. I promise."

"I do trust you, Tourmaline," said George. "And you've done some amazing things, but ... how can you be sure?"

Tourmaline thought for a moment. "Because," she said slowly, "I know what my magic is now. All of it."

George's eyes widened.

Tourmaline took a breath. "And if I know how it works, and I'm not fighting against it and it's part of me – like my mother said it is – then I can use it. I can use it to protect us if I need to. And I won't let anyone make us do anything we don't want to do ever again. Not even Captain Violet."

"What *is* your magic, then?" asked George.

"How did you figure out how it works?" asked Mai.

"It started in the little library place next to the boardroom, when all the books went extra bookish," said Tourmaline. "I accidentally touched them after I used the magic key. My hands didn't glow and I didn't mean to, but I made all that chaos happen with magic. It's just like the postcard said – 'the Museum of Marvels can give you the rest'. And it has."

She looked at George. "And then I thought about your experiments and how you wrote everything down and how you always asked *why*. And so I asked, but why?"

There was a pause.

"It's because," said Tourmaline, "I am a Source."

Three pairs of brown eyes blinked at Tourmaline while everyone thought about this.

George took a breath and said, very seriously and with a sense of wonder, "I get it. You aren't just a magical artefact, like the people at the market thought. And you don't just amplify magical artefacts. The Source made you the same as it is. You *are* a Source."

Tourmaline smiled at her friend. It felt right. It felt true. "I *do* amplify magical artefacts, like you said at the Dark Market. But it's not all I can do." She looked at her hands. "When I touch a magical artefact and I make it *more*, my hands glow, just like the Source." They did look just like the Source when they glowed, that oil-on-water slick of colour kaleidoscoping around under her skin.

"And when I touch something that *isn't* already a magical artefact, like those books, my hands *don't* glow. But I *turn* them into magical artefacts. I think maybe I can make anything a magical artefact."

George's face had opened up. "Yes!" he said. "That's why you never glowed with the fan or that hat at the market, but you *did* at Winona's stall and with the key. Every time your hands didn't glow, you were using magic anyway, you were making an ordinary thing into a magical artefact."

"I wonder," said Tourmaline, "if the glowing isn't the magic working, it's just the magic trying to tell me something – trying to tell me how it works – but I wasn't listening before. I was trying to stop it." A smile spread slowly over Tourmaline's face. "Maybe I just have to go with it."

George smiled back. "But you can *control* it, though. The lucky coin wasn't lucky before you used it to open the tent. It worked because you needed it to."

Tourmaline looked down at her hands. It did all make sense, except she was still a bit worried about one thing. "What do you think about the times I really didn't want my magic to do anything at all, and it did? Like at Winona's stall at the Dark Market. It's got us into so much trouble."

"I wonder," said George, "if it's like when I'm very nervous about saying the wrong thing and I think about it so much it sometimes comes out anyway."

"You mean I was wishing so hard that my magic wouldn't do anything to give me away ... that I actually made the opposite thing happen?"

George stuck his hands in his pockets and smiled at his friend. "I think so."

"But," said Tourmaline, "what about when I really wanted it to work, like when we did your experiments, and it just wouldn't?"

"Did you really, truly want it to?" asked George. "Or were you actually a bit scared that it would?"

Tourmaline bristled a little. "Well, not *scared*, George."

"A bit concerned, then," said Mai.

"A little bit, maybe," said Tourmaline. She didn't have to think about this for very long. It all felt right, like the fit of her hand in her mother's, or getting told off by Josie for eating biscuits in her bed when they both knew perfectly well that she wasn't going to stop.

"Thank you, George," she said, happy that they'd solved one of the problems they'd set out to solve when they'd left Pellavere. It seemed fitting that it had happened just as they were about to find out the other thing that Tourmaline most wanted revealed – who knew her secret? Who had sent the postcards?

She turned to the door. "I think I know what to do now."

She put her hands on the door and solemnly thought about the door-ness of it. How it wanted to open and close. How that was what it had been made for. The purpose of the door was to open, and the purpose of the mechanisms on it was to make that happen. She thought hard about this happening ... and it happened.

The mechanism started moving, silently, levers sliding, cogs turning all the way down the door.

"I'm not sure I'm going to get used to that," said George.

"I'm not sure either," said Tourmaline.

"Are we going in?" asked Celandine, pushing forwards.

"Wait," said Tourmaline. She turned round to look at her friends. "Let me go in first. I just want to ... I need to..."

"You want to see who it is first?" asked Mai.

Tourmaline nodded. "That. And also if it's a trap or if it's someone really dangerous I could try to use my magic to protect us, so it's best if you're behind me."

"But—" Celandine wasn't looking very happy. She was fidgeting and her gaze kept darting to the door.

"I think it's a good idea," said Mai. "We'll be right behind you."

Tourmaline took a deep breath and faced the door, and opened it, just a bit.

She stepped through.

There was a pause and an intake of breath.

"You!" said Tourmaline.

Chapter
Twenty-nine

George looked at Mai and then Celandine, his eyes wide. Whoever was in there, Tourmaline recognized them.

"I knew you'd come, Tourmaline," said a voice from beyond the door. It was a man's voice. A voice George recognized.

He pushed through the door in alarm, closely followed by Mai and Celandine.

Tourmaline was standing inside the room, a deep scowl on her face. "You don't know anything about me," she said.

"Don't I?" asked her father mildly.

It was Evelyn Coltsbody.

Inside the room, there was a cell. It was clear, like

the tank the octopus had been in, but much bigger. And inside the cell, Evelyn Coltsbody. Sitting there on a wooden chair with a small table in front of him. There was a newspaper on it, which he had evidently just placed down. There was a bookcase behind him and he was dressed in his explorer's clothes. He had his legs crossed, looking as though he were in a comfortable hotel enjoying his holiday.

"*You* sent the postcards?" said George.

"And you've brought your friends, of course." Evelyn Coltsbody smiled at Tourmaline. "I knew if I sent you that postcard, you'd figure it out and go to the Dark Market. And then when you got the next postcard, you wouldn't be able to resist working out the next puzzle and acting on it."

"I don't have to behave how you think I will," said Tourmaline crossly. It was especially frustrating that her father was absolutely right, so the only thing she could reasonably do was deny it.

But Evelyn just laughed softly. "How did you enjoy the market?" he asked. "And the Museum of Marvels? It's quite something to behold, isn't it? Talk to me,

Tourmaline. I'd love to hear all about your adventures."

Tourmaline didn't say anything for a moment. She was tired and hungry and quite fed up, as well as being outraged and shocked and disappointed. She was also curious, in spite of herself. But she had her magic to protect her. And he was quite safely locked away in the cell.

Finally, she opened her mouth. "Adventures?" she said. "Well, let's see. We've been locked up in a tent, locked up in a lab and almost disappeared out of existence because of you. Not to mention kidnapped and then nearly *double* kidnapped by rogue hunters."

"And yet you've escaped every time," said Evelyn, unperturbed.

"That's not the point!" said Tourmaline. "We've been all over Escea and we had to learn to fly in a magical airship and then Captain Violet tried to—"

"But it sounds as though you've had a fantastic time," said Evelyn.

Tourmaline gave up. Partly because there was no winning an argument with someone like Evelyn who went into it thinking they were right and had no intention of being persuaded otherwise. And partly, she had to admit, because he *was* right. She'd had an undeniably marvellous adventure, even if it could have done with more cake.

"What do you want?" she demanded.

Evelyn regarded Tourmaline. She lifted up her chin and tried to look imposing.

"I would have thought that was obvious," he said.

"Well, it's not," said Tourmaline. Her heart was beating fast. She wasn't sure if she really wanted to know the answer. Or possibly she just wasn't sure what she wanted the answer to be.

Evelyn looked at Tourmaline thoughtfully for a few seconds before he spoke. "You, Tourmaline, are an adventurer," he said. "Your mother is an adventurer. And so am I. It's in your blood, no matter which way you look at it."

Tourmaline opened her mouth, and Evelyn held one hand up. "I know. You're nothing like me and you don't have to do anything you don't want to do."

Tourmaline allowed herself a small glower at Evelyn. "Go on, then," she said shortly.

"I sent you the postcards," said Evelyn, very slowly and deliberately, "because I want you to hunt with me."

Tourmaline blinked. And had some feelings. A rush of shock, followed by a deep sense of pleasure that her father wanted to hunt with her. After that, there were several memories of the terrible things he had done, followed by substantially fewer memories of the less terrible and possibly helpful things he had done.

Evelyn leaned his hands on his knees, his eyes bright, his face alive. "Haven't you had the most wonderful adventure following the clues on the postcards?" he asked. "That doesn't have to end, Tourmaline! Wouldn't you like to see the world?"

"Yes," said Tourmaline. "I mean, no. I mean, not with you. Not if you want to march into places that don't belong to you and start taking over."

"Also," she said, before he could start talking again, "you're in the AICMA's custody for trying to steal things like whole islands. Which is why you won't be hunting anything anywhere any time soon and it's all your own fault."

Evelyn smiled a smile that almost had Tourmaline

looking over her shoulder in alarm, except that she didn't trust him enough to take her eyes off him.

"Wait a minute," said George. "How did you even send the postcards to Tourmaline?" He edged cautiously into the room.

"I have friends, George. And plenty of people who are willing to work for me, for a price."

"Was it Captain Violet?" asked Mai. Nobody would have put it past the captain to work for him when it suited her only to decide that Winona's offer for Tourmaline was more profitable. She'd worked with — and betrayed him — before.

Evelyn almost laughed. "No, not on this occasion," he said.

He inspected his nails. "Now, be a dear and get me out of here before any agents arrive. I know you can do it." He looked up at her meaningfully. "I know about your abilities, Tourmaline."

Tourmaline scoffed loudly to cover up the fact that a tiny bit of her had believed that he really wanted to hunt with her. And that an even tinier bit had been pleased about that.

"So *that's* why you really wanted me to come here?" she said. Her father knew about her magic and he wanted her to use it to help him.

Evelyn just regarded her steadily.

"How did you know?" Tourmaline asked quietly.

"It was obvious from the minute I saw you in the cavern on the island," said Evelyn.

"But how?" Tourmaline asked again. How could he have known something so important about her when she hadn't even known it herself at that point?

"Several things," said her father. "For one, there was a rope on the ground right next to the Source. Then there was a wet blanket, even though you yourself were dry. You also looked a lot cleaner than the last time I had seen you in the centre of the maze, so between those three things it stood to reason that you had fallen into the Source. I might have asked about it at the time if I hadn't been completely frozen and unable to talk." Here, he frowned at Mai, who lifted her chin and smiled.

"Also," Evelyn continued, "it was you holding the cat, Fitzsimmons, that got us away from the Source in the end, and it got me to thinking about what the Source might have done to you. I tested my theory with the first postcard I sent you, and found it was true. You saw the picture of the Dark Market and you went there." He regarded Tourmaline levelly. "I'm right, aren't I? You can make any magical artefact work, better than it ever did before."

Tourmaline glanced at George. That wasn't all she could do. She could make things into magical artefacts all on her own, even if they'd never been near the Source. But of course no one there was about to tell Evelyn Coltsbody that.

"I'm not getting you out of there," said Tourmaline. She folded her arms.

Evelyn smiled. "Very well. But think about it, Tourmaline. You and me, side by side, exploring the magic of the entire world! I've learned about some wonderful places during my delightful stay with the Agency." He looked at Tourmaline as though assessing what effect his words were having on her. "I thought we could start with the Midnight Islands."

There was a pause. A long pause where Tourmaline

thought about the intriguing sound of the Midnight Islands and the possibilities that came with the wind in her hair as she sailed on a ship or flew through the clouds looking down on the wonders below.

"What do you say? Simply set me free a little earlier than the Agency would like."

"Tourmaline." George nudged her arm.

She shook her head hard. "No," she said.

Evelyn shrugged. "That's quite all right, Tourmaline. I understand. If you won't do it, your sister will. Celandine?"

Chapter
Thirty

Celandine darted forwards and before Tourmaline could even blink in shock, the other girl – her *sister*? – had slipped her hand into the pocket where Tourmaline had put the magic key, pulled it out and darted away.

Tourmaline didn't even move. Her mind was reeling. Sister? She didn't have – had never had – a sister. She looked at George. He was staring, wide-eyed, at Celandine. Mai's mouth was open.

"Half-sister," said Celandine. "Obviously." She lifted her pointy chin and planted her feet apart.

The stunned silence continued.

"Perhaps," said Evelyn, "this is a topic to be discussed later."

"I think it's a topic to be discussed exactly now," said

George, putting his arm around Tourmaline.

Mai suddenly clapped her hand to her mouth, then un-clapped it and pointed at Celandine. "Back in the boardroom when we were reading the AICMA's list and there was a bit torn off the bottom. *You* tore it off. It was *your* name on the list! It was Celandine Coltsbody!"

"I *knew* something was going on with her," said Tourmaline now that she could speak again and was feeling justified in never having trusted Celandine in the first place. "And now it all makes sense, because she's *his* daughter."

"So are you!" Celandine retorted.

"I can't believe I saved you from the nothing," said Tourmaline. "It was *you* sending those postcards for him all along and you never said a word."

Celandine scoffed. "Like you'd have listened to me if I'd tried to explain."

"Now, now, children. That's no way to talk to your sister. Either of you," said Evelyn. He seemed to be enjoying himself tremendously.

Tourmaline gave him the most furious of all her glares.

"Oh, don't be cross, Tourmaline. You needed help with your magic, didn't you?"

"I didn't need anything from you!" she said, even more annoyed because she really *had* needed help, desperately. And what was worse, everywhere she had been and everything she had done since getting the first postcard and leaving Pellavere actually *had* helped her learn about her magic. She never would have found out what she could do and why, and how it all worked, if she'd stayed at home and not embarked on another adventure.

"Well?" he asked. "Did you find out everything you wanted to know?" The way he was smiling indicated that he already knew the answer.

Tourmaline scowled.

"I'll take that as a yes, and an admission that I did, in fact, help you," said her father. "And now you've helped me," he continued. "Isn't it wonderful how families work? Celandine, would you mind?" He gestured to the glass wall of the tank or cell or display case – whatever it was he was imprisoned in. "The door is over there."

Celandine stepped to the door with the magic key in

her hand. The lock was as clear and transparent as the cage itself and when she put the key inside, it looked as though it was hanging there, about to unlock absolutely nothing.

"He's not *supposed* to escape!" said Tourmaline.

"And were you *supposed* to go to the Dark Market to learn about your magic?" Evelyn asked with a raised eyebrow. "Were you supposed to know where the AICMA headquarters are and waltz right into their museum? What about going off to save your mother from the island of Elsewhere? Were you supposed to do that?" He shook his head. "Where would Persephone be now if you only ever did what you were supposed to do?"

"That's not the— What I did isn't the same as— You make it sound as though—" Tourmaline gave a loud huff. Her father was, infuriatingly, right.

But Evelyn had turned his attention to Celandine. And the key that wasn't working.

"Celandine?"

The girl looked worried. "It's not doing anything. I can't make it work."

She turned to Tourmaline and Tourmaline recognized the expression on her face. Celandine looked exactly how Tourmaline had *felt* when she first saw her mother trapped in the cavern on the island of Elsewhere.

Evelyn had been in the AICMA's custody for weeks now. Which meant that Celandine hadn't seen her father in weeks. Longer than Tourmaline had been without her mother when she had disappeared and before Tourmaline had found her again.

She knew exactly what Celandine was feeling. But she was feeling it for Evelyn Coltsbody, and he was nothing like Persephone Grey.

"You rescued your mother when she needed it," said Evelyn, looking at Tourmaline.

"But she's not you," said Tourmaline.

"Because she has adventures where she finds artefacts, takes them and brings them back to the university so that they can put them in glass cases," said her father, quite reasonably, which made Tourmaline suspicious.

"Whereas I," Evelyn continued, "have adventures

where I find magical artefacts and take them and bring them back for myself so that I can put them in glass cases." He spread his hands to indicate the glass cell. "Irony aside, we're not all that different. Your mother wanted to take something from the island of Elsewhere and so did I, and yet here I sit, while she continues to use magical artefacts for her own ends. Tell me, Tourmaline, how is that fair?"

"My mother is a good person!" Tourmaline said, with the particular defensiveness of someone who is defending a parent. She reserved the right to complain about Persephone if she ever felt the need, but she had no intention of letting anyone else do it – *especially* not Evelyn Coltsbody.

"And couldn't I be a good person? With you by my side?" asked Evelyn. "Both of you, my two daughters."

Tourmaline opened her mouth, then closed it, then opened it again. She looked at Celandine and had the most extraordinary set of complicated feelings. They were a blend of resentment and wonder and kinship and disbelief and annoyance and something like being deeply pleased, but not that, not that at all.

Then Celandine cried out, "It's working!" and the key opened the door to Evelyn's cell or tank or whatever it was. He stood up in an unhurried way, as though he were leaving the country club after dinner, and strolled right out as George clutched Tourmaline's arm.

Evelyn took out a pocket watch (Tourmaline assumed it was a non-magical one since the Agency had surely confiscated all magical artefacts from him) and glanced up as though he were expecting rain.

Tourmaline glanced up too, with a frown, and suddenly something crashed into the roof above them. She flung her arm out, grabbing Mai (George was already glued fast to her other side) and ducking as the something made an immense noise – a smashing and grinding and grating, as though it were ripping off the whole roof.

Chapter Thirty-one

It was only when the grinding noise stopped that Tourmaline looked up. Mai stood next to her and she pulled up George. They stared at the ceiling.

"What was that?" Tourmaline demanded. But the cell was empty. Celandine and Evelyn had strolled right past and out of the door.

Tourmaline ran after them, Mai and George following.

The air outside was full of dust, the ground littered with crumbled brick. As they passed the threshold of the building, it flickered into sight again and they could see that the something had demolished part of the roof.

The something was now casting a large, ship-shaped shadow on the clearing.

"It's *The Mermaid*!" said Mai, and then sneezed three

times. "They couldn't see the building so they drove straight into it."

"I think that's my cue to leave," said Evelyn pleasantly. "Thank you so much for your help, Tourmaline. I truly appreciate it." He smiled. "As I hope you appreciate mine."

Two ropes dropped down from the side of the ship. Evelyn started climbing one of them, Celandine swarming much faster up the other one next to him.

At the top, where the ropes had come from, a face appeared, framed by black braids and topped by a large black hat.

Captain Belvedere. She nodded at Tourmaline as though they hadn't recently both been involved in a lengthy and dangerous chase that could have resulted in a long fall and a crash, or a further kidnapping.

"You shot cannonballs at us!" she shouted up at the captain.

"But we didn't *hit* you," said Captain Belvedere. "We were trying to capture you, not blow you out of the sky, remember?"

"That's hardly any better," said Tourmaline, scowling.

"You were going to take me back to the Dark Market."

"Was I?" asked the captain.

There was a pause, then Tourmaline's scowl opened up into surprise. "Wait a minute, Captain Belvedere. You wanted to bring me here? For him?" She jerked her chin at her father, who was now at the top of the rope and swinging himself aboard the ship.

"Not *for* him," said Belvedere. "That makes it sound like I work for him, which I don't. I work for myself. It also makes it sound as though it were for some terrible reason, instead of your father wanting you to join him. And while we're talking about family, you should probably stop calling me Captain Belvedere and call me Cathryn instead. I am your stepmother, after all."

Tourmaline stared at the captain. "You're Celandine's mother?"

Celandine was now standing next to Captain Belvedere and Tourmaline could see the resemblance – that same defiantly pointed chin.

"Celandine's mother, Tourmaline's stepmother," Cathryn said, as though it were perfectly simple.

And with that, she gave a salute and the ship rose

into the air leaving Tourmaline blinking and spluttering. Her curls blew back in the draught and she stared up at the three figures leaning over the side of the ship. Evelyn Coltsbody, Cathryn Belvedere and Celandine.

A family. *Her* family? It was such a big idea she sat down straight away on the grass.

She didn't even notice what George had seen – that Persephone had just entered the clearing on a motorcycle.

George nudged Mai hard – there was someone sitting in the green sidecar, her black hair streaming back under her safety helmet. It was Mai's mother, Emiko Cravenswood. He peered anxiously past them for any other vehicles following and was relieved to see that it was just two mothers and not three, his own being mercifully not present.

"Come on," he said to Mai. They both rushed off to intercept Persephone and Emiko, who had a lot of questions and concerns to voice. These were followed by a lot of exclamations and queries concerning the state of the AICMA headquarters (which was still visible since the children were so close to it), not to mention the fact that *The Mermaid* was slowly rising into the sky with an escaped prisoner on board.

Tourmaline heard George and Mai talking over Persephone and Emiko's questions and glanced over her shoulder. Persephone was wrestling with the goggles and cap she had been wearing, trying to disentangle them from the mass of her curls.

Tourmaline looked back up at the ship, now looming above her.

"Something to think about, Tourmaline," her father called down. And he dropped something over the side of the ship. The something was a rectangle of card and as it fluttered down through the air, twisting this way and that, she saw that it was a postcard.

She jumped up and snatched it out of the air.

"Goodbye for now, Tourmaline!" called Celandine. She waved, and the look on her pointed little face had so much hope in it that Tourmaline found herself waving back.

"Tourmaline!" called Persephone, having finally managed to disengage herself from the goggles and from Mai and George.

Tourmaline turned to face her mother, slipping the postcard into one of her pockets just in time for Persephone to barrel into her with a hug that she returned just as fiercely.

Chapter
Thirty-two

Tourmaline stifled a yawn as she looked out of the motorcar window. Mai's head was sinking closer to the other window. George was in the middle, already asleep with his head on Mai's shoulder.

It was night outside, the dark countryside lanes winding their way back to Pellavere. Persephone was driving and, next to her, Emiko was listing (in a low voice so as to not wake George) the many problems that the AICMA were going to have to deal with now that their headquarters was uninhabitable, most of it having been destroyed by a flying ship or some other mysterious means. Tourmaline ducked her head when this came up since she was the mysterious means that had done most of said destroying.

"Nearly home," said Persephone, glancing over her shoulder and smiling at Tourmaline. Emiko turned back too and checked Mai with an eagle eye.

Up ahead, the university loomed, cutting a dark, turreted silhouette into the chocolate sky. It was a return to something known, when everywhere else had been new (and exciting, but also occasionally terrifying). But she felt different upon this return. She *was* different – and not just because she understood her magic now, but because adventures change a person.

She glanced round the motorcar – Persephone hunched over the wheel, Emiko still talking about the uncertain future of the Agency, Mai now as deeply asleep as George.

She slipped the last postcard, the newest one, out of her pocket. It was blank on the picture side. Tourmaline tucked it almost right under her leg and ran one glowing finger over the white card. Like a magic painting revealed by water, a tower appeared. It was tall, built of sandy blocks, with ramparts curving up around its sides, almost like a helter-skelter slide. Its narrow windows suggested it had many floors, and on the bottom of it was a sign next to a closed door.

Tourmaline squinted to make out the writing on the sign. It said:

MIDNIGHT TOWER
The library of Everywhere

Her heart beat faster and she fidgeted in her seat. Another quick, guilty glance at Persephone and she turned the postcard over. There was no poem, no riddle, only two lines that made her knees jiggle and her sense of adventure fizz.

The biggest hunt is yet to come.

Your move, Tourmaline.

Look out for
Tourmaline's next
adventure, coming
Spring 2025!

Q&A with Ruth Lauren

What are the Tourmaline books about?

The first book is about a very determined girl who has to launch a rescue mission when her intrepid explorer mother goes missing. After that, we follow Tourmaline and her friends on a dangerous chase across the magical world as she learns about her own place in it, and about a part of her family that she never knew she had. And finally, Tourmaline has to venture farther than she's ever gone before in a desperate attempt to save her home – and possibly even the whole world!

The series is also about friendship and thinking about right and wrong and how it's not always straightforward to tell the difference. It's about who decides ownership of artefacts – magical or otherwise! And it's about how we relate to family and what our place is in the world. But first and foremost, it's about exploring and adventure.

Tell us a bit more about the world?

Tourmaline has lived all of her life in Pellavere University where her mother works as an artefact hunter, but after her mother goes missing, she ends up sailing the seas, discovering a very strange island and learning that magic exists. Tourmaline's world becomes a lot bigger and more magical than she ever thought was possible. She learns that there are all sorts of people and places in the world, and that she wants to discover and explore all of it. Book three will give her more than she bargained for in that department!

What are you most excited to share with readers?

I really hope readers will love Tourmaline and her friends (and possible foes) and I can't wait for them to follow her on her adventures as she travels to new, magical – and sometimes perilous – places.

I'm also excited to share the beautiful and striking covers by artist Sharon King-Chai. They're stunning!

What books that inspired and entertained you would you recommend to readers?

So many! I'll restrict myself to a few favourites I've read recently. For the most wonderful fantasy, I love the Utterly Dark series by Philip Reeve, the Monsters of Rookhaven books by Pádraig Kenny, *Gallant* by V.E. Schwab and *Nura and the Immortal Palace* by M.T. Khan. Give the Strangeworlds Travel Agency series by L.D. Lapinski a try if you like adventurous travel! The Five Realms series by Kieran Larwood is brilliant. Anything by Lucy Strange is fantastic, as is anything by Hilary McKay. I love the Eerie-on-Sea Mysteries by Thomas Taylor.

This year, I enjoyed *Ellie Pillai is Brown* by Christine Pillainayagam, *The Cats We Meet Along the Way* by Nadia Mikail, and anything and everything by Katya Balen. I'll leave it there or I'll be recommending books forever.

Any tips for aspiring writers?

Read. Read everything. Read all the time. Nothing will make you a better writer than reading. And when you start writing, keep going. If you want to be a writer, you have to be very persistent and never give up – a bit like Tourmaline!

Acknowledgements

First, thanks to my insightful and gracious agent, Anne Clark, whose ideas about my manuscripts inspire me to make them better.

Thanks to my editor, Mattie Whitehead, whose unfailing enthusiasm for Tourmaline is a delight.

To the whole team at Little Tiger for being the perfect champions for the series and lovely people to boot and to Nina Douglas for publicity and kindness.

Thanks again to Pip Johnson and Sharon King-Chai for respectively designing and illustrating another beautiful book. I only did the words – the reason it looks so good is all them!

To Bolinda and Stephanie Lane for such a wonderful audio-book version, and to my German publisher, Fischer. I love that Tourmaline is available in these forms.

To the bloggers, teachers, librarians and reviewers who read and cheered and put the series in the hands of children. To the lovely authors who so kindly blurbed. And to the booksellers who were unfailingly polite as I bumbled my way through signing stock. If you meet a bookseller, just know that they are automatically a nice person.

Thanks to my family – my husband, Dave, and my kids, who will now have a book dedicated to each of them so no arguments.

Last, but definitely not least, thanks to Michelle Krys, for all of the things.

About the Author

Ruth Lauren lives in the West Midlands in England with her family. When she isn't writing, she's almost certainly reading, playing D&D (badly) or falling down the rabbit hole of whatever she's currently obsessed with. Ruth's acclaimed middle grade novel *Prisoner of Ice and Snow* was chosen by the American Booksellers' Association as a top debut of the season, and its sequel *Seeker of the Crown* earned a starred Kirkus review.

𝕏 @ruthlaurenbooks | 📷 @ruthlaurenbooks